ISABEL FELT THE URGENCY IN HIS KISS

But she held back, frightened of letting down the defenses she had built over the years.

"You should know this," he said. "I wanted you from the first moment I set eyes on you."

"You did?" she breathed as her mouth opened under the pressure of his. Suddenly nothing else existed in the world except Leo's hands touching her, his mouth caressing her. She felt passion rising in her like the spring tide until a small whimper formed deep in her throat.

"Isabel." It was a love word, a caress, a promise.

"Yes," she whispered, "oh, yes. . . ."

JOAN WOLF is a native of New York City who presently resides in Milford, Connecticut, with her husband and two children. She taught high school English in New York for nine years and took up writing when she retired to rear a family. She is the author of four other Rapture Romances, *Summer Storm, Change of Heart, Beloved Stranger,* and *Affair of the Heart.*

Dear Reader:

We at Rapture Romance hope you will continue to enjoy our four books each month as much as we enjoy bringing them to you. Our commitment remains strong to giving you only the best, by well-known favorite authors and exciting new writers.

We've used the comments and opinions we've heard from *you*, the reader, to make our selections, so please keep writing to us. Your letters have already helped us bring you better books—the kind you want—and we appreciate and depend on them. Of course, we are always happy to forward mail to our authors—writers need to hear from their fans!

Happy reading!

The Editors
Rapture Romance
New American Library
1633 Broadway
New York, NY 10019

PORTRAIT OF A LOVE

by

Joan Wolf

RAPTURE ROMANCE

NEW AMERICAN LIBRARY

PUBLISHER'S NOTE

This novel is a work of fiction. Names, characters, places, and incidents either are the product of the author's imagination or are used fictitiously, and any resemblance to actual persons, living or dead, events, or locales is entirely coincidental.

SIGNET, SIGNET CLASSIC, MENTOR, PLUME, MERIDIAN
AND NAL BOOKS
are published by New American Library,
1633 Broadway, New York, New York 10019

First Printing, November, 1984

1 2 3 4 5 6 7 8 9

PRINTED IN THE UNITED STATES OF AMERICA

Chapter One

❦

Isabel MacCarthy turned off Interstate 95 to Route 26, the road that would take her into Charleston, and as her rented station wagon hummed along, she looked forward with a mixture of anticipation and apprehension to the job ahead of her. Commissioned to paint the portrait of South Carolina Senator Leo Sinclair, Isabel had received her first commission, a big break for her, and she was nervous.

She was tremendously fortunate to have gotten this chance. Gabe Bellington, the *Times* art critic, had recommended her to Mrs. Sinclair, the senator's mother, and Isabel had been hired on the strength of that recommendation. Hired at a fee that had made her blink, Isabel had only just begun to make a name for herself in the art world, and was not yet accustomed to commanding decent, let alone princely, sums of money.

This commissioned portrait was a big chance for more reasons than the money, however. Leo Sinclair was probably one of the most-well-connected men in the United States. He was a figure in the worlds of society, sports, and politics. If he was pleased with her work, this portrait could be

Isabel's entrée into the buying circles of the wealthy. Or so Isabel was devoutly hoping as she drove east on this lovely March afternoon.

Having read up on Charleston in the New York Public Library before she left, Isabel was delighted and charmed to see that the books had not exaggerated the city's beauty. New York had been damp, raw, and windy, but here the sun was bright, the air pleasantly cool, and the gardens were aflame with flowers. Marvelous houses with airy galleries Charlestonians call piazzas were grafted onto genuine Georgian and Federal style residences.

The Sinclair house proved to be larger than many of the surrounding homes. It was set back from the street behind a wrought-iron fence and the piazza ran across the front of the house rather than down the side. Isabel parked her car and got out, stretching muscles that felt decidedly cramped after an all-day drive. She glanced down at her slacks and thought she looked distinctly out of place in the middle of this charming eighteenth-century street. She was wearing tan corduroy pants and a burgundy crew-neck sweater. Isabel was partial to reds and burgundies because she thought they were a good foil for her black hair and olive-toned skin. Reaching into the car for her purse, she closed the station-wagon door and started purposefully up the path toward the entrance of the Sinclair house. Whenever Isabel was nervous, the expression on her face was aloof and rather severe, and today was not an exception. She lifted the door knocker and waited.

A distinguished-looking black man opened the door.

"Hello," said Isabel coolly. "I'm Isabel Mac-Carthy. I believe I'm expected."

The man opened the door wider in welcome. "Come in, Miss MacCarthy. I'll tell Mrs. Sinclair you're here."

"Thank you," Isabel replied gravely, and stepped into a center hall that was right out of the eighteenth century.

"This way," the man said as he led her into a drawing room of Georgian perfection. Isabel was looking at the tiles on the fireplace when she heard someone enter the room from behind her.

"Those are Sadler tiles," a soft Southern voice said. "How do you do, Miss MacCarthy. I'm Charlotte Sinclair."

Isabel turned and saw a thin, white-haired woman dressed in a simple dark-blue dress. She was smiling and holding out her hand, and Isabel's face softened slightly as she took the slender, blue-veined hand into her own firm, competent grip.

"How do you do, Mrs. Sinclair. This is a very beautiful room."

The older woman's skin was so fine and fair that it almost looked translucent. Her bones were still beautiful and she must, Isabel thought, have been absolutely smashing when she was young. Mrs. Sinclair was of medium height and held herself erectly. She smiled serenely up at Isabel, who was a few inches taller, and said, "You must be tired after such a long drive. Come upstairs to the family sitting room and I'll give you some tea."

"I left my things in the car," Isabel began.

"Simon will get them and put them in your bedroom." Mrs. Sinclair started to walk toward the door but suddenly halted. "Would you *like* tea?" she asked. "We can have coffee if you would prefer it."

"Tea will be fine," Isabel said, and followed her hostess back over the huge Oriental rug, which she judged to be authentic and priceless, and into the hall.

They went up the stairs, through an arched door in the second-floor hallway into one of the most beautiful rooms Isabel had ever seen. Completely paneled in natural cypress, the room was mellow and warmly glowing in the late-afternoon light. The woodwork was magnificent, with carved pilasters, fretwork, and decorated moldings done in darker pieces of mahogany.

The room, stunning as it undoubtedly was, did not look like a museum. The chairs and sofa were contemporary and comfortably upholstered in a slightly faded chinz. The small tables held lamps, an assortment of priceless china, books, and magazines. It was obviously a room that was lived in.

Mrs. Sinclair gestured Isabel to the sofa, which was placed at a right angle to the fireplace. Isabel sat down and kept her back very straight, determined not to be intimidated by the beauty and wealth that surrounded her. Tea was brought in by a middle-aged black woman. The service, Isabel noticed as her hostess poured, was silver and antique—probably Georgian.

"Lemon?" asked Mrs. Sinclair. "Sugar?"

"Nothing, thank you." Isabel accepted her cup and sipped. The tea tasted very good.

"You *are* a tea drinker," Mrs. Sinclair said approvingly.

Isabel looked at her and met a pair of smiling blue eyes. She felt herself relax a little.

"I'm Irish," she said. "I was brought up on tea."

"You don't look at all Irish," Mrs. Sinclair said. She put down her teacup. "Now, doesn't that sound narrow-minded? Do forgive me, my dear. I really didn't expect you to have red hair and freckles."

For the first time Isabel smiled. "I'm what they call the black Irish," she said. "It comes from all those Spanish sailors who were shipwrecked on the Irish coast during the Armada. My mother's family was from Kerry—she looked even more Spanish than I do."

Mrs. Sinclair chuckled, a charming sound that somehow put Isabel even more at her ease. "You look very lovely, my dear. And very young. I must confess I had not expected you to be so young."

"I'm twenty-six," said Isabel coolly.

Mrs. Sinclair gave her an amused glance. "Well, of course, that probably sounds quite old to you," she murmured tactfully.

Isabel suddenly grinned. "It sounds quite ancient, actually. But you're right, Mrs. Sinclair, I *am* young. I thought you had understood that from Mr. Bellington."

"What I understood from Gabe, my dear, was that you are extraordinarily talented."

Isabel had never been any good at accepting compliments. "I hope you won't be disappointed," she said a little gruffly.

Mrs. Sinclair turned to look at her. "Let me tell you about my conversation with Gabe. I called him to say I had persuaded Leo to have his portrait painted and that I was looking for a painter who was a realist yet also an artist. I don't have anything in this house that isn't quality, and if I wanted just a likeness of Leo, I'd have his picture taken. I don't need a society portrait, but I want a portrait that looks like him. I don't want him ending up with an eggplant for a nose." Mrs. Sinclair was not smiling now. "Gabe suggested you almost immediately. He had seen a show of yours recently and was very impressed."

"Yes. It was my first show, actually. Mr. Bellington was very kind." Isabel was serious as well. "I did abstracts while I was in art school, Mrs. Sinclair, but I have always been drawn to realism. And I like doing portraits; I had two of them in my show, in fact. I think I can do something that will please Senator Sinclair."

Mrs. Sinclair made a rueful face. "Senator Sinclair, I regret to tell you, is completely uninterested in having his portrait done. He is only doing this to please his poor doddering old mother."

"Oh," said Isabel, a little disconcerted by this news. She had been expecting a willing subject.

"Do you see that picture?" Mrs. Sinclair said, gesturing to the portrait over the mantel.

"Yes." Isabel looked at the distinguished and aristocratic face of an elderly gentleman in eighteenth-century clothes.

"That is James Sinclair, Leo's great-great-great-grandfather. He was an officer in George Washington's command and the man who built this house."

"I see," said Isabel softly.

"This house is filled with such portraits, Miss MacCarthy. The Sinclairs built this house and have lived in it ever since the end of the eighteenth century. Leo is not unique in this family; he is only the latest in a long line who have faithfully served their state and their country over two centuries. I want a portrait of him to hang on my walls."

"I understand."

Mrs. Sinclair gave Isabel a smile of great beauty. "And of course, he is my beloved son and I dote on him—but don't tell him that, will you?"

Over dinner that evening Isabel met the other members of the Sinclair household. The senator, she had been told by his mother, would arrive from Washington the following day.

Isabel's bedroom on the third floor of the house was furnished with a four-poster bed that Mrs. Sinclair had described as a field bed, along with a Queen Anne wing chair and table. Over the fireplace hung a portrait of Mrs. Sinclair's great-aunt, who, as Isabel was informed, had been a devoted worker in a Columbia hospital for Confederate wounded.

Feeling a little overwhelmed by all the family history, Isabel put on a wine-colored paisley print shirt dress—one of the three dresses she had brought with her. Dinner, she felt, would be a more formal occasion at the Sinclairs' than it was in her own apartment back in New York. She changed the thin gold rings in her ears for a wider, more dressy pair and then surveyed herself in the large cheval mirror in the corner of her room.

Her hair, which was her one vanity, was very long, reaching almost to her waist. It was thick and black with a texture like heavy silk. She had secured

it off her face tonight with two tortoiseshell bar-
rettes and her dark-brown eyes, set under straight
black brows, looked gravely back at her from the
mirror. Isabel was elegantly tall and slim, though
her nose was too long and her skin too sallow. She
shrugged. Oh, well, it wasn't her picture that had to
be painted, she thought philosophically and went
downstairs to the dining room.

At dinner she met Senator Sinclair's younger sister and brother.

"So you're the painter who's to do Leo's portrait,"
Ben Sinclair said, giving her a friendly grin. He was
about twenty-four, tall, blond, good-looking, and
confident. "Lucky Leo," he said. "Mama, can't I
have my portrait painted?"

"When you become a senator," his sister
retorted. "And I wouldn't hold my breath until that
happens!" Paige Sinclair turned to Isabel. "Don't
pay any attention to Ben, Miss McCarthy."

Ben laughed and softly replied and Isabel sat and
listened to the play of talk around her, watching,
assessing, judging, and occasionally contributing
something when the conversation demanded it of
her.

She was among people who were completely for-
eign to her. Senator Sinclair's fair-haired, elegant
sister, a senior at Charleston's exclusive Ashley Hall
Day School, was utterly removed from the girl Isabel had been in high school. Both of these young
Sinclairs had an easy self-confidence, a natural
patrician gloss that Isabel had noticed in many of
the people who browsed through the gallery at her
New York show two months ago. Their every ges-
ture bespoke Money, Family, and Social Eminence.

Isabel felt like a creature from another planet in their midst.

"You're very quiet, Miss MacCarthy," Ben Sinclair said.

"I'm just feeling a bit overwhelmed by all these blond good looks," she replied a little dryly.

Ben laughed, obviously pleased, and Paige said with amusement, "Wait until you meet Leo, Miss MacCarthy. You haven't seen anything yet."

"Children, stop teasing Miss MacCarthy. Come along with me, Isabel, and I'll show you around the rest of the house." Mrs. Sinclair started toward the door.

Paige groaned dramatically. "Now you're in for it, Miss MacCarthy. She's going to show you the plate that was buried during the War Between the States."

"And the portrait of Czar Nicholas that the czar himself presented to our revered ancestor who was an ambassador to Russia," chimed in Ben.

"And the clock that belonged to the ancestor who was a cavalry hero in Lee's army," chanted Paige.

"I shall be delighted to see all of those things," Isabel said firmly.

"A tea drinker and an antiquarian," Mrs. Sinclair said. She gave Isabel her lovely warm smile. "You're a girl after my own heart, Miss MacCarthy."

Isabel smiled back. It was impossible not to respond to this charming woman. "You called me Isabel a minute ago," she said.

"So I did. Well, come along, Isabel, and I'll give you the penny tour."

"Now, Mama, it's worth more than that. How

much does the Charleston Historical Society charge these days?" Ben queried wickedly.

His mother ignored him and ushered Isabel across the hall and into the downstairs drawing room.

Chapter Two

❧

Isabel did not sleep very well, even though she was tired from the long drive. She knew what was keeping her awake, but was incapable of doing anything about it. Quite simply, she was nervous about meeting Leo Sinclair tomorrow, especially since she had learned he was not enthusiastic about having his portrait painted. If she were to do a good job, Isabel needed his full cooperation.

She was afraid Leo would turn out to be an older, smoother version of his brother, Ben: aware of his own charm, a little spoiled, a little selfish. He was extraordinarily good-looking; she knew that from the photographs she had seen. Yet what Isabel looked for in a face was not good looks but that elusive something one could only call character. She would love to do a portrait of Mrs. Sinclair and would find it difficult to do Ben. She was beginning to fear she would have trouble with Leo.

The senator's credentials would lead one to believe him the last of the Renaissance men. He had been an outstanding college-football player; in fact, he had won the coveted Heissman Trophy as the best college player of the year. Although he had been the number-one draft choice in the NFL and could have commanded a huge sum of money to sign a football contract, Leo Sinclair had accepted a three-year Rhodes scholarship and gone off to Oxford, where he took a degree in History.

Returning home after his Oxford sojourn, he signed to play for the Dallas Cowboys. For four years he had been All-Pro and had three times been to the Super Bowl.

When Leo's knees had given out, he had campaigned for the Senate, and had won handily. South Carolina was distinctly enthusiastic about Leo Sinclair, and the chances looked good for him to become a fixture on the national political scene. He was thirty-four years of age. And unmarried.

How could he help but be complacent? Isabel thought, tossing restlessly in her antique bed. He was the man who had everything. And he had it effortlessly, it seemed. Everyone loved Leo Sinclair; he was the original Golden Boy. Isabel, who had had to fight hard for every break she ever had, was very much afraid she was not going to like the senator at all.

She looked over the house in the morning and decided to set up her easel in the library, where the early light was excellent. Isabel preferred to work in the morning. Mrs. Sinclair was completely agreeable; Isabel was to consider the house at her disposal.

Neither Paige nor Ben had been at breakfast when Isabel ate. Paige was at a tennis lesson, Mrs. Sinclair said as she poured coffee, and Ben had gone to work.

"He's taken over at the development office," his

mother informed Isabel with noticeable pride. "Ben has his father's head for business. He's only been there two years, since he left college, but he's taken hold wonderfully."

"Your husband was one of the first people to see the resort potential of the Sea Islands, wasn't he?" asked Isabel.

"Yes. He built Island Views you know. It was the pioneer resort and retirement community in the area. He did very well with it," Mrs. Sinclair said with truly monumental understatement. Isabel knew from her reading up on the family that Charles Sinclair had parleyed his inherited forty-five hundred acres of seafront property into a resort that had made him millions.

"Ben is interested in real estate and development, then," Isabel said politely.

"Yes. He's going to develop one of the islands off Island Views next." Mrs. Sinclair sipped her coffee. "As I said, Ben is very like my husband."

"And Leo?" asked Isabel in a carefully neutral voice.

Mrs. Sinclair's face broke into its lovely warm smile. "Leo," she said, and her voice was very soft, "Leo is Leo and like no one else in the world. You'll see. He'll be here after lunch."

Later in the morning Isabel went out for a walk. The city enchanted her, for she felt as if she had been whisked back to another, more gracious time. She walked slowly, enjoying the sunshine, the flowers, and the old houses with their great verandas.

It was early spring and there were many other tourists around. Isabel's tall slim figure attracted a

great deal of attention, though she was unaware of
this interesting phenomenon. She was an unusually
striking girl, with her long ebony hair and dark
intent face in vivid contrast to the bright scarlet of
her sweater. She moved among the crowd of tourists, absorbed, aloof, and alone, not noticing the
interested and admiring glances that followed her
along the narrow streets of old Charleston.

She was gone for longer than she had planned,
and when she arrived back at the Sinclair house, it
was to find that the senator had arrived. Simon
practically beamed as he informed her of this fact,
and she climbed the stairs to the second-floor drawing room valiantly trying to ignore the flutter in her
stomach.

He was sitting and talking to his mother, but he
stood as soon as Isabel entered the room.

"Leo, this is Isabel MacCarthy," Mrs. Sinclair
said. "Isabel, allow me to introduce my son."

"Miss MacCarthy," Leo Sinclair said as he came
forward to take the hand she offered.

Isabel had been prepared for the Viking good
looks. She had, after all, seen numerous photos of
the senator. But she had not been prepared for the
quality of his presence.

"How do you do, Senator," she said, she hoped,
calmly, and looked up into his face. His coloring
was amazing, she thought. Thick blond hair was
like a golden helmet; his eyes shone like twin sap-
phires. Unconsciously, her own eyes narrowed. He
wasn't at all pretty. Indeed, the impact he made on
one was thoroughly male.

"Were you out seeing the sights of the city, Miss
MacCarthy?" he asked. His voice was distinctly

Southern: gentle, slow, and drawling. It also sounded faintly amused.

Isabel realized she had been staring and felt her cheeks grow a little warm. "Yes," she said, and looked determinedly at his mother. "I'm afraid I rather lost track of the time."

"That's quite all right, dear," Mrs. Sinclair said. "Leo and I have been so busy talking that the time quite flew. Have you had lunch? Shall I order tea?"

"I haven't had lunch," said Isabel, "but I'm not hungry, Mrs. Sinclair, really."

"Well, I am, Mama," said the senator.

"Didn't they give you lunch on the plane?" his mother asked with a little frown.

He grinned, a slow smile that brought a look of lazy sunshine to his face. It was a marvelous smile, thought Isabel, her eyes once again on Leo Sinclair. "Yes," he said.

Mrs. Sinclair laughed. "Sit down, Isabel, and I'll order tea."

Isabel complied, taking a wing chair by the beautiful carved chimneypiece, and Leo sat down on the sofa next to his mother. Isabel's observant eyes noted that he moved with extraordinary grace for so big a man.

"You drove all the way down from New York, Miss MacCarthy?" He pronounced it "New Yawk."

"Yes, Senator. I thought I'd see a little bit of the country while I had the chance."

He smiled at her. I can't wait to paint this man, Isabel thought and smiled back. "I don't blame you," he said.

Simon came in with the tea try, and as she

poured, Mrs. Sinclair told her son that Isabel had decided to work in the library.

"Fine." The deep soft voice took on a note of affectionate teasing. "Do you want me to dress up in eighteenth-century garb, Mama?"

"Of course not. You will wear . . ." Mrs. Sinclair broke off and looked at Isabel. "Whatever shall he wear, Isabel? A business suit is much too dull." She looked at her son doubtfully. "Your dinner jacket, perhaps?"

He gave her a reproachful look. "Mama. Please."

His mother shrugged helplessly and two pairs of blue eyes turned to look at Isabel. Isabel didn't think it mattered very much what he wore, really, but obligingly she put her mind to the problem.

"Something blue," she said after a minute. "A sweater, I think. I'll do you standing in front of the mantelpiece."

"Standing," said Leo resignedly. "Oh, well."

"You can wear your blue V-neck sweater," his mother said. "Isabel is right. It will be a good foil for your eyes."

Leo looked amused and ate one of the sandwiches Simon had brought with the tea.

"Delicious," he said, and held the plate out to Isabel. "Have one, Miss MacCarthy."

Isabel accepted. The sandwich was crabmeat and it was delicious. Isabel took a hungry bite.

"I can stay until Thursday," Leo said, and Isabel put her sandwich down abruptly and stared at him.

"Thursday? But today is Saturday."

"Won't that be enough time, dear?" asked Mrs. Sinclair worriedly.

Isabel was really upset. "Of course it won't be

enough time. I need at least two weeks of sittings if I'm to do a portrait."

"Well, I cannot give you two weeks." The senator's voice was quiet but firm. "Congress is in session and I must be in Washington." He turned to his mother. "I'm sorry, Mama."

Hell, Isabel thought explosively. Bloody bloody hell. Her face, however, showed none of her agitation; when it came to concealing feelings, Isabel was an expert.

"I was not aware, when I accepted this commission, that your time would be so limited, Senator," she said now in a cool, clipped voice. She looked directly into the astonishing blue eyes of the man seated opposite her and thought, you bastard. You're just like the rest of your kind. What do you care that I've come all this way for nothing? It's not convenient for you to sit for your portrait, and that's that.

"You don't work from photographs?" he asked her.

"No."

The blue eyes moved from her face to his mother.

"This is all my fault," Mrs. Sinclair said in obvious distress. "I should have thought of this sooner."

Leo shrugged, his big shoulders moving easily under his expensive jacket.

Damn, thought Isabel.

Leo looked at her. "Well, Miss MacCarthy," he said in his soft voice, "I reckon you'll just have to come back to Washington with me."

Isabel's dark eyes widened. "Washington!" she said in astonishment.

"Yes, Washington. I have a house in Georgetown and there's plenty of room. I can give you a few hours every morning." He cocked a golden eyebrow. "What do you say?"

Isabel took a deep breath. She had not realized how much she wanted to do this portrait. "I say it seems I don't have a choice in the matter," she answered.

He grinned at her. He was a devastatingly good-looking man. "Not if you want to paint my portrait, you don't."

He probably mowed down women by the dozens with that smile, Isabel thought. She looked back at him a little austerely.

"Really, Leo, will it be proper?" Mrs. Sinclair asked worriedly. "I'm afraid I simply cannot accompany you at this time."

"Mama," said Leo affectionately, "how I love you. It will be perfectly unexceptional, I assure you. Of course, I reckon I could always hire a duenna . . ."

Mrs. Sinclair laughed as she was meant to. "How absurd you are, Leo. Well, if you're sure . . ."

"I'm sure," he replied firmly, and Isabel realized with a flash of amusement that Mrs. Sinclair was far more worried about her son's reputation than she was about Isabel's.

Leo met Isabel's eyes and divined, instantly, what her thought was. His blue eyes laughed at her, although his face remained grave. "Well, Miss MacCarthy? Are you willing to chance it?" he asked.

Isabel leaned back in her chair. "I want to paint

your portrait, Senator," she said pleasantly, "and, so I will come to Washington with you."

Over dinner that evening Isabel got a chance to see the entire Sinclair family in action. Leo's father, she knew from her reading, had been killed in a plane crash three years earlier, so it was just Mrs. Sinclair and her three children.

Isabel sensed very clearly that the four of them were indeed a family. It had been a long time since she herself had experienced anything like the casual, comfortable family atmosphere that prevailed at the Sinclair dinner table. They sat there, blond and beautiful, rich and privileged, and Leo, at the head of the table, outshone them all. It was difficult to relate to people who had been so blessed by the gods, Isabel thought wryly.

"We'll have our coffee in the drawing room," Mrs. Sinclair said as she rose gracefully from the table.

"Cal and I are going to a party at Kathleen's," Paige reminded her mother.

"Ah ha," said Leo good-naturedly. "Cal. Now that's a new name. Who is he, Paige? And what happened to Johnny Montgomery?"

Paige laughed at her big brother as they left the dining room, and for a moment Isabel felt a stab of sharp envy for this lovely, self-assured girl who had brothers to tease her and protect her. When Cal, a slender, brown-haired, polite boy, arrived, Leo left the drawing room to see them out. When he returned, there was a slight frown between his brows.

"What's the matter?" his mother asked imperturbably. "I've found him to be a nice boy."

"He is nice. I just hate to see her getting into a car with a teenage driver, that's all." He gave his mother a half-humorous look. "I'd be a terrible father. I hate to let go."

Mrs. Sinclair sighed. "I know. But Paige is a sensible girl. She knows she can call anytime, and either Ben or I will come and get her. I think she has enough sense not to get into a car with a boy who's been drinking."

"I hope so," said Leo, and for the first time there was a look of grimness around his firm, well-cut mouth.

Ben put down his coffeecup. "Well, I'll be on my way too," he said, and stood up. He grinned down at the relaxed figure of his brother. "If Paige calls, you're on duty tonight. I have a date with Susan Deboise."

"Well, well, well," Leo drawled. "You're more faithful than Paige, little brother. Am I going to be called on to be best man one of these days?"

"I'm thinking about it," Ben said. "If I wait for you to make the jump first, I'll be old and gray."

Leo's blue eyes glinted. "Give my regards to Susan," he said.

"I'm not letting you near Susan," his brother retorted. He bent over to kiss his mother and smiled at Isabel as he left the room.

"He sounds serious," Leo commented to his mother after Ben was safely down the stairs.

"I think he is. Susan is a lovely girl, and she's good for Ben."

Leo nodded absently and his eyes focused on Isabel, who was sitting next to the chimneypiece. She was wearing a soft wool dress of pale gold, and his eyes lingered for a minute on her long, elegant legs before moving thoughtfully to her face. Isabel saw the look and, to her own surprise and discomfort, felt blood come into her cheeks. Annoyed at herself, she sat up straighter in her chair. Good God, she thought, you'd think a man had never looked at my legs before. It was a moment before she realized he was smiling at her.

"I'm so much older than my brother and sister that sometimes I get fits of paternal instinct," he said.

"There must be ten years between you and Ben," she managed to say.

"Yes. And sixteen years between me and Paige."

"I had quite given up on having another child when Ben came along," Mrs. Sinclair said. "And Paige was a complete surprise."

Leo put down his coffeecup and leaned back on the sofa, stretching the muscles in his back. His darkly clad shoulders looked enormous against the paler upholstery of the sofa. "What about you, Miss MacCarthy? Do you have brothers and sisters?"

Isabel had never realized how charming a Southern accent could sound. "No," she answered simply, though her own voice sounded unpleasantly nasal and clipped in contrast to his. "I was an only child." The blue eyes were steady on her face and she found herself continuing, "My mother died when I was thirteen."

"Oh, my dear," said Mrs. Sinclair in quick sympathy.

"And your father?" asked Leo.

Unknown to her, Isabel's face took on the bleak look it always wore when the subject of her father arose. "My father died three years ago," she said, and looked at her hands.

"That's when my father died," Leo said quietly.

Isabel took a deep, steadying breath. "It was not a good year," she said, and looked up from her lap and met his eyes. They were the most absolutely blue eyes she had ever seen. It was not until Mrs. Sinclair spoke that she was able to look away from him.

"Do you want to start painting tomorrow, Isabel?" the senator's mother asked.

"How can I?" Isabel asked in genuine bewilderment.

"Can't you start the portrait here?"

"Oh, I see what you're thinking." She shook her head. "The light would be different."

"Then you'll have to wait until you get to Washington."

"I'm afraid so," said Isabel a little apologetically.

"Good," said Leo Sinclair unexpectedly. "That will give me a few days to show you around the area."

Isabel tried to speak coolly. "You needn't worry about entertaining me, Senator."

His smile was warm and his slow voice held a hint of amusement. "It's not a worry," he said easily. "It will be a pleasure."

"What Mass do you want to go to tomorrow, Leo?" asked Mrs. Sinclair.

"The ten-thirty, I reckon."

Mrs. Sinclair nodded and looked at Isabel. "Would you like to come with us, Isabel?"

Isabel hadn't been to Mass in years and she looked in surprise at the two Southern aristocrats in front of her. "I thought Sinclair was a Scottish name," she said, following her own line of thought.

"It was originally Saint Claire—French," Leo replied. The lamp on the table next to him had been lighted and a soft glow fell upon the smooth golden wing of his hair. "My ancestors were Huguenots fleeing from religious persecution, and for centuries the Sinclairs were staunch Protestants. Until Mama came along and subverted the whole lot of us." He turned to smile at his mother, and his hair shimmered in the light. "Lady Marchmain," he said to Mrs. Sinclair in a gentle, teasing voice.

"Don't link me with that horrible woman." Mrs. Sinclair shuddered. "Did you see *Brideshead Revisited* on television, Isabel?"

Isabel shook her head, and her own black hair shimmered against the pale gold of her dress. "No. But I read the book."

"Amazing," Leo said. "She read the book. No one reads the book anymore, Miss MacCarthy. They watch the movie or the TV show."

"I'd rather read the book," Isabel said.

"Why?"

Isabel looked at him thoughtfully. "A movie can only show you characterization through action— what a person says and does. A book can open up the whole interior life of a character to you. It's a question of depth."

"I see. And is that what you try to capture in a portrait, something of the interior life of your subject?"

Isabel was startled. "Why, yes."

"I shall have to watch out, then, or you will discover all my deep dark secrets."

"Do you have deep dark secrets, Senator?"

He smiled at her faintly. "Ah," he said, drawling a little more than usual, "now that is something you will just have to find out."

Chapter Three

Isabel excused herself from Mass the following morning but the entire Sinclair family got into Ben's car at ten-fifteen and left for church. They did not return home until almost twelve-thirty.

"Leo was holding court," Paige told Isabel with a laugh.

"More people wanted to know my thoughts about the trade Dallas just made than wanted to consult me on senatorial matters," Leo said good-naturedly as he held the door for his mother.

"My, but it's warm," Mrs. Sinclair commented as she entered the drawing room, where Isabel was sitting comfortably with a book.

"I know." Isabel put her book down. "And it was so cold and damp when I left New York that I didn't think to bring any warm-weather clothes with me." She was wearing her tan corduroy pants with a pin-striped man-tailored shirt. "A heat wave must have rolled in overnight."

"It feels marvelous to me," Paige said.

"After lunch," Leo told Isabel, "I'll take you out to Island Views, if you like. The beach there is lovely." He was wearing a lightweight gray suit and he looked healthy and distinguished, masculine and elegant, all at once.

"It's super," Paige said enthusiastically. "May I come too, Leo?"

Her brother looked at her. "Did I ask to come along with you last night?"

Paige looked nonplussed and Isabel felt the color sting her cheeks. "I told you not to worry about entertaining me, Senator," she said quickly.

"And I told you I never worry," Leo replied serenely.

Mrs. Sinclair chuckled. "Do go with him, Isabel. If you're going to paint his portrait, you're going to have to get to know each other."

This was indisputably true, and after a minute Isabel nodded. But when Paige said wickedly, "Look out, Miss MacCarthy, he's broken half the female hearts in America," Isabel thought to herself, Not this heart he won't. Her heart had been given away long ago—to a stretched canvas and a palette of oil paints. So she merely smiled slightly at Paige and accepted Mrs. Sinclair's offer of another cup of coffee.

An hour and a half later they were driving down the coast in Mrs. Sinclair's Buick. "It's about an hour's drive to the beach," Leo told her comfortably.

Isabel turned her head to look at him. He had changed out of his suit into a navy Izod shirt, khaki pants, and sneakers. The short-sleeved shirt made him look very strong. Isabel stared for a moment at his bare arm and then focused on his profile.

"Are you active in the development office as well, Senator?"

"Please call me Leo." He gave her a quick, sideways glance. There was a look of humor about his mouth. It was a wonderful mouth, thought Isabel. She would have to try to catch that feeling of humor. "After all," he continued, "we're going to be living together for several weeks."

Ah, thought Isabel, I'd better get this clear straight off. "In one sense only," she replied calmly but firmly.

There was a brief silence. Then, "Of course," he said, his voice slower and softer than usual. "I'm sorry if you thought I meant to imply something more."

All of a sudden Isabel felt very silly. "Sorry if I seemed to overreact," she said a little gruffly. He smiled but made no reply. "And please," she went on carefully, "won't you call me Isabel."

"Isabel." He drawled it out in his gentle way, and for the first time in her life Isabel found herself liking the sound of her name.

"Well, to answer your question," he began, "no, I'm not active in the family business. Ben is the one who inherited my father's talent in that area." He shook his head a little in admiration. "He's quite something, you know. Has a mind like a razor."

"You can't be any slouch yourself," Isabel said with raised brows. "Rhodes scholarships aren't handed out to the average student."

"I was lucky," he said amiably.

There was a pause and then Isabel changed the subject. "Your mother has her heart set on this portrait," she said.

"I know. She's pestered me about it ever since I got elected." A small smile creased the corner of his mouth. "Ever since she married my father, she's become more Sinclair than the Sinclairs."

"She certainly is proud of the family."

"She certainly is." The note of amused affection was clear in his voice.

"She's a lovely person," Isabel heard herself saying.

"They broke the mold the day they made my mother," Leo Sinclair said simply, and Isabel turned to stare at him again. It sounded so odd, so old-fashioned to hear a man saying such a thing of his mother. I suppose, Isabel thought with a flash of insight, it's only men like Leo Sinclair who can afford to say things like that. No one in his right mind would ever accuse the senator of being a mama's boy.

An arched bridge crossed the water to Island Views, the famous Sinclair-built modern resort and retirement community. Isabel was wide-eyed at the sight of the beautiful homes, the yachts, the four golf courses and seventy tennis courts.

"It's fabulous," she said as they walked along a quiet stretch of beach that faced the house the Sinclairs had retained for their own use. She laughed. "I suppose this is what life in the Sunbelt is all about."

"It is for a lot of people," he replied. "Do you play golf, Isabel? Or tennis?"

"No." A lovely breeze blew off the water and stirred the hair at her temples. She had plaited the length of it into a long thick braid that fell down her back almost to her waist. She looked out at the blue water and smiled a little ruefully. "I grew up in New York City—and *not* on the fashionable East Side. Our big sports were stoop ball and basketball in the schoolyard."

"Stoop ball?" he said in bewilderment.

Isabel looked at him and suddenly smiled, not her usual, social smile, but a real one, rarely seen and radiantly beautiful. "You have to be from New York," she said.

He was watching her face. "I have found," he said, "that New Yorkers are absolutely the most insular people in the entire world."

Isabel laughed. "You're probably right."

"Do you mind sitting on the sand?" he asked.

"Of course not." Isabel dropped to the white sand and clasped her arms around her knees. Leo stretched out beside her, his arms behind his head, his eyes narrowed against the sun.

"How did you get into art?" he asked half-sleepily.

"My high-school art teacher encouraged me, mostly. She was super. If it weren't for her, I would never have gone on to art school."

"Why not?"

Leo's soft, sleepy sounding voice disarmed Isabel. If she had thought he was conducting an inquisition, she would have frozen up, but she answered easily and truthfully, "We couldn't afford it. Money was always tight in my house."

"But you did go to art school."

"Yes. I got into Cooper Union." She rested her cheek on her updrawn knees. "It's a terrific school in New York City that gives degrees in architecture, engineering, and fine arts. And the tuition is free."

"Free tuition. You can't beat that."

She laughed. "No. And if it weren't for Mrs. Simpson, I would never have known about it. As it was, I got four years of first-class training."

"And now you are on the road to success."

She sighed. "I hope so."

A comfortable silence descended between the two of them. Isabel thought Leo had fallen asleep. The sun was warm and she opened another button on her shirt. She had rolled up her sleeves before they left Charleston. She gazed out over the water and felt the warmth sinking into her. It was very peaceful. After a few minutes she turned to look at the man sleeping at her side. He was so beautifully blond, she thought. His lids opened, and eyes blue as the cobalt sky above looked into hers. Isabel felt her heartbeat accelerate.

"I was falling asleep," he said.

"Don't mind me."

He smiled and sat up effortlessly. He was very close to her, a fact that did nothing to slow the wild tapping of her heart.

"Washington is so hectic that I really appreciate a chance to just relax."

"I know what you mean." Isabel hoped her voice sounded normal. "New York is like that, too."

He was looking at her slender brown arm revealed by the rolled-up sleeve of her shirt. He reached out with gentle fingers and touched her forearm.

"How did you get that?"

He ran his finger along a thin, whitish scar that looked as if it had been there for many years. Isabel cleared her throat. "I fell when I was a child. On glass." She turned her eyes away from him, fearing the sensations his touch awakened in her.

He looked for a minute in silence at her averted head, so beautifully and proudly set on her long neck.

"Look," he said suddenly. "Over yonder."

Isabel followed his pointing finger to a sea bird in full flight carrying a fish in its long orange beak. "It's a royal tern," Leo said. "Their nesting grounds are all over the Sea Islands."

"It's lovely," said Isabel. He stood up and she followed his lead gratefully. It made her uncomfortable to be so close to him. "Do you play golf and tennis?" she asked as they resumed their interrupted walk.

"I golf some," he replied. An indefinable change of expression crossed his mouth. Isabel suddenly remembered why he had left football. He had had several operations on his knees, or so she had read in a sports magazine.

"Football isn't kind to knees," she remarked neutrally.

"No."

Isabel glanced at him walking beside her. His hands were in his pockets, his blond head bent a little forward. He sounded perfectly normal.

"I have never understood this urge men seem to have to knock each other about," she said astringently. "It makes no sense at all."

"I suppose it doesn't—to women at least."

"What a condescending remark!"

He stopped walking and turned to look at her. "Yours was scarcely complimentary," he said, and raised his golden eyebrows.

After a minute Isabel laughed. "I suppose it wasn't. All right. About football, let us simply agree to disagree."

"I've gotten used to people disagreeing with me," he said good-naturedly. "The senate does that for you."

"Do you like it?" she asked curiously. "Washington and being a senator, I mean."

"Yes," he answered promptly. "Mama would say it was in the blood, that Sinclairs were born to govern."

He slowly walked forward again and Isabel fell into step beside him.

"Perhaps I should paint you holding a sceptre and a crown."

"Don't be funny," he said as he took a hand out of his pocket and gave her braid a good hard tug.

"Ouch!" said Isabel, and stared at him reproachfully.

"I couldn't resist," he said with cheerful unrepentance. "I've been longing to do that all day. I've felt just like a little boy in the fourth grade ever since you appeared with that enticing braid hanging down your back."

Isabel's face lit with its rare sweet smile. "Shame on you, Leo," she said. "And to think it's the likes of you who run this country."

"I'm better than a lot of them," he said imperturbably. "And we're making progress. You finally called me Leo."

Isabel smiled and they continued to stroll along the beach, each savoring the view.

"This place is absolutely fabulous," Isabel said again as they got into the car to leave.

Leo started the motor. "I know. But I wouldn't want to live here."

"Why not?"

"It's too easy, too lazy. There's nothing to challenge you, nothing to throw your mind into."

"I see what you mean," said Isabel. They were on the main road when she asked, "Do you enjoy a challenge, Leo?"

"It's meat and drink to me. It's what I liked about Oxford and about football."

"Oxford and football," said Isabel. "What a combination."

"It's not so unusual," he murmured. "Only at Oxford they call it rugby."

"And now you find your challenge in the Senate."

"Yes." He glanced at her, a fleeting flash of blue. "What about you, Isabel? Do you find painting a challenge?"

"Not exactly," she said slowly. "I do it because, well, because I have to. But you're right in one sense. It is a struggle to paint well."

There was a thoughtful pause. "Yes," he said then. "How did you get into doing portraits? I rather thought serious artists didn't do them anymore."

"For a long time they didn't. Everything was abstract. The invention of the camera changed things so much, and representational painting seemed passé. But Abstract Expressionism has lost a lot of its force. There's been a renewed interest in realism since, oh, the fifties, really. And a portrait—a good portrait—is much more than just a record of how a person looks. At least, I think it is."

"Anyone whose seen a portrait by Rembrandt would have to agree with you."

Isabel laughed. "I can hardly put myself in the same class as Rembrandt. But, yes, that is precisely what I mean."

Leo changed the subject. "I'm very sorry about the inconvenience of making you come to Washington. I reckon neither Mama nor I thought too much about how much time you would need." A faint smile touched his lips. "The photographic mentality," he said.

Isabel shrugged. "It's all right. You must know that doing this portrait is a big break for me." She turned her head. "I'd go to Antarctica with you if I had to."

His blond hair blew in the breeze from the open window. The expression on his face was inscrutable. "Would you?" he said. "That's nice to know." A wary expression came over Isabel's face and after a minute he went on easily, "Coming to Washington might actually be a good idea. I'll introduce you around—'Isabel MacCarthy, the portrait painter,' that sort of thing."

His tone of voice was comical and Isabel relaxed. "And I can hear the answer already. " 'Isabel *who?*' "

"Then I'll say, 'Isabel MacCarthy. From New York. My mother engaged her on the recommendation of the *Times* art critic to do my portrait. We shall be having a party when it's finished—you must come.' "

"A party," Isabel repeated blankly.

"Certainly. You must know that Washington spends half its time looking for excuses to have parties. There are dinners and receptions every night of the week. I save a fortune on food by dining out. So I'll introduce you around," he repeated. "Then Mama will come up and hostess a big unveiling party for the portrait and *voilá*, you're in business."

Isabel's head was in a whirl. "Are you serious?"

"Perfectly. There is, however, one condition."

"What is that?"

"The portrait had better be good."

"Yes," Isabel said faintly as she leaned back against the cushion. "It had better be, hadn't it?"

Chapter Four

❧

Isabel's mind was a jumble of thoughts as she went to bed that evening. Could Leo have been serious? Did he really intend to launch her into Washington society?

"The portrait had better be good," he had said. Certainly, Isabel thought as she lay sleepless on her antique four-poster bed, she could not have found a better subject for her first commissioned portrait. Leo Sinclair had a face any artist would give his right arm to paint.

He had extraordinary coloring, so fair and yet so vivid. She would paint him with the light striking his hair, she thought. The features of his face, so strong and yet so good-humored, reminded her of a man well-accustomed to having the world go his way. He was golden and royal, just like a lion, she thought. Isabel smiled to herself in the darkness. Of course. Leo the lion. And on that thought, she fell asleep.

Leo was reading the newspaper at the breakfast table the following morning. He looked up as Isabel came in, and he lowered the paper a trifle. "Good morning," he said.

If Isabel had a fault, it was that she was too serious. She had grown up a solemn and responsible only child and had never learned the trick of light-hearted teasing. But now, looking at Leo as he sat in the sunny breakfast room, his eyes very blue in the morning light, she felt an unusual surge of gaiety.

"Good mawnin'," she replied demurely, and sat down at the table.

Simon came in to ask what she wanted to eat and Leo said, "Miss MacCarthy is making fun of my accent, Simon."

"It's not you that has the accent, Mr. Leo," Simon replied.

Isabel laughed. "*Touché*, Simon."

The black man asked her for her order and left the room. Being waited on by black servants made Isabel extremely uncomfortable. Simon hardly seemed like a humble Uncle Tom type; in fact, Isabel had heard him and Leo laughing and arguing in the kitchen after dinner last night. Yet there was just something a little pre–Civil War about it all.

"I'm getting spoiled," she said lightly. "I'm not used to servants at home."

He looked at her shrewdly. "Do you think Simon is our resident slave?"

She flushed. "Of course not."

Leo stirred his coffee. "Would it surprise you to learn that Simon has one grandson at MIT and another at Stanford?"

Isabel stared at her own coffee and then bravely looked up to meet his eyes. "Yes, it does surprise me," she said honestly. "And it is my turn to beg your pardon for being insulting."

His mouth remained gave, but a slow smile crept

into his eyes. For what seemed like a very long moment they just sat there looking at each other, the blond, blue-eyed man and the dark, intense-looking woman. When Mrs. Sinclair entered the room, the intangible something that had been floating in the air between them dissipated.

"Good morning," Leo's mother said cheerfully.

"Good morning, Mama," said the senator.

"Good morning, Mrs. Sinclair." This time Isabel spoke the words in her own accent. Leo cast a swift, amused glance in her direction before he asked if he could pour his mother some coffee. Simon came in with Isabel's breakfast and some melon and toast for Mrs. Sinclair.

"I think we'll head back to Washington tomorrow, Mama," Leo said as his mother sipped her coffee. "Isabel is anxious to get to work. And so am I, for that matter."

"All right, dear," Mrs. Sinclair said tranquilly. "Will you drive up in Isabel's station wagon?"

"Will that be all right with you, Isabel?" Leo asked.

"Of course."

Mrs. Sinclair smiled at Isabel. "Leo told me last night about his idea of introducing you around in Washington. I must say, I think it is a splendid notion. And we'll have a nice party to unveil the portrait."

"I don't know what to say," Isabel stammered. "It's very kind of you both to trouble yourselves over me."

"Nonsense. It's no trouble at all. In fact, it's time Leo had a party of his own. He's been dining out for two years now."

"There's nothing like being a Southern Democrat in Washington these days," Leo said to Isabel. "The Democrats wine and dine me because they need my vote to defeat the President's programs in the Senate, and the Republicans wine and dine me because they need my vote to pass them." He grinned. "As a result, I'm on the receiving end of a constant flow of invitations."

Isabel's dark eyes sparkled a little. "And how do you usually vote?"

He buttered a piece of toast. "Sometimes for, sometimes against. It depends on the particular piece of legislation."

"An independent man, in fact."

"I reckon."

"Isabel, dear," Mrs. Sinclair said softly, "what kind of clothes do you have with you?"

"Oh." Isabel wrinkled her long, narrow, and elegant nose. "No dinner dresses, that's for sure. I wasn't expecting to make the social scene."

"Of course you weren't. I really think that you should regard the Washington engagements as an investment, though. It may cost you a few dresses, but the benefits could be considerable. There are a lot of art patrons in Washington."

Isabel frowned thoughtfully. "True. I do have a couple of dresses home in New York. A friend of mine belongs to a very stuffy architectural firm and I always have to make a good impression at their dinners." She looked abstractedly into space. "I could call Bob and have him send the dresses to Washington, I guess. They'd be a start."

There was a pause. "Why don't you do that?" Mrs. Sinclair said then, very gently. Leo said noth-

ing. "If you like, we can do some shopping this afternoon," Leo's mother added.

Isabel, thanks to the check Mrs. Sinclair had sent
her for one-half of her commission, had a very
healthy bank balance at present. However, unless
she got a few new commissions or made a few good
sales, that money was going to have to last for a long
time. Mrs. Sinclair was right. At this point, a few
dresses would be a wise investment. But she had to
make it very clear to the senator that the only
reward he was going to get for his efforts on her
behalf was a portrait.

"I'd like that," she replied to Mrs. Sinclair. "But
will your local stores take a check on a New York
bank?"

"I'll put them on my charge," Mrs. Sinclair said.

"All right. Then I'll make the check out to you."

"That will be just fine, dear."

"Don't you have a MasterCard or a Visa?" asked
Leo. It was the first he had spoken since she had
mentioned Bob's name.

"No. I learned long ago that if I couldn't pay cash
for it, I couldn't afford it."

He raised a golden eyebrow. "Very wise." He
pushed his chair back and stood up. "Mama will
give you my Washington address and phone number so you can make your arrangements." He
looked at his mother. "I've got a few calls to make
today, Mama. I should be home for dinner."

Mrs. Sinclair held up her face for his kiss and
smiled at his back as he walked out of the room.
Then she turned back to Isabel. "I think we'll go
first to a nice little boutique I know," she said, and
for the next fifteen minutes the two women dis-

cussed clothes and acted for all the world as if a man named "Leo Sinclair" did not exist.

After breakfast Isabel put in a call to New York.

"Mr. Henderson's office," an efficient female voice said when she had gotten the extension she asked for.

"Hi, Marion, it's Isabel. Is Bob in?"

"Isabel." The woman sounded surprised. "I thought you were in South Carolina."

"I am and this call is costing me a fortune." Isabel had put the charges on her home phone. "Is he there?"

"Give me your number and I'll have him call you right back," Marion said practically.

"Great," said Isabel, and gave her the number and promptly hung up. Barrows, Barrows, Dunlop, and Shore could afford the call more than she could, she thought.

In three minutes the phone rang. She picked it up and said, "Hi, Bob."

"Hi yourself. What's up? You haven't run into any trouble, have you?"

"No. In fact, things are looking pretty good. The senator has to go back to Washington and I'm going to do the portrait there. *And* he's going to introduce me to some people in the hopes I can drum up some more business."

"Hey, Isabel, that sounds great!" Isabel smiled at the genuine enthusiasm in his pleasant tenor voice. "Are you calling to give me your new address?"

"Yes. Do you have a pen? Okay." She gave him the address and phone number, then added, "And I want you to send me a couple of dresses, Bob. You know, the ones I bought for the Christmas and the president's parties last year. The black-and-gold ones."

"Oh, yeah. Are they in your closet?"

"Yes, in the garment bag in the corner."

"Okay. How about shoes?"

"Good thought. Better send me the gold sandals. They're in one of the shoe boxes in the closet."

"Will do."

"How are you surviving, Bob? Are you eating properly?"

He laughed. "I'm eating out. Those TV dinners you left me are wretched."

"I know," she said sympathetically, but didn't ask him who he was eating out with. She had long ago perfected the art of keeping out of Bob's private life.

"I miss you," he said unexpectedly. "The apartment seems damn empty."

"That's a nice thing to say," she replied softly.

"I mean it. Well, I'd better not run up this bill any more or old Barrows will want to know who my client is in South Carolina."

"Okay. Take care of yourself. I'll be home in a few weeks."

"Right. And I'll get these things off to you right away."

"Thanks. 'Bye for now."

"Good-bye, Isabel."

Isabel hung up the phone and sat staring at it for a few minutes as she visualized the curly brown hair, clear, intelligent hazel eyes, and warm smile of the man who was perhaps the best friend she had ever had. What would he do, she wondered, if she moved out of the apartment? Then, startled by her own thought, she stood up. She had no intention of moving out on Bob. She couldn't imagine what had even put the thought in her head. She smoothed down her hair and went into the drawing room to wait for Mrs. Sinclair.

The shopping expedition was a success, and Isabel, to her surprise, enjoyed it very much. She had grown up without knowing the pleasure of shopping for clothes with another woman. She supposed her mother must have taken her shopping when she was younger, but she didn't remember it much. What she remembered about her mother were the years of sickness. During her teen years, there wasn't any money for cozy shopping expeditions. All Isabel remembered from those times was the constant battle to get enough money out of her father to pay the rent and utility bills and buy some food before he drank all his salary up in the local bar.

"This was fun," she said to Mrs. Sinclair as they sat in a small restaurant sipping tea. "I don't often shop like this. There's no occasion to, really. I practically live in jeans and sweaters."

"You have the kind of figure that looks marvelous in anything, my dear," Mrs. Sinclair said with a smile.

"You're very kind." Isabel changed the subject. "Do you want a full-figure portrait of Leo?"

"I don't know, Isabel. What do you think?"

"I think I'd like to do it full-length," Isabel said slowly. Her eyes were slightly narrowed as she imagined the pose she had in her brain.

"You must do it as you think best. I'm sure what-ever you do will be marvelous."

Isabel looked at the older woman a little wryly. "Such absolute confidence makes me a little uneasy, Mrs. Sinclair."

"It shouldn't. And you have a perfect subject for your first big commission, you know." Mrs. Sinclair looked at her and said comically, "It simply isn't possible, my dear, to make Leo look *bad*."

Isabel's face suddenly broke into its magical smile. "And here I was thinking that your confi-dence was in me."

The older woman's eyes were bright. "I have con-fidence in you both, my dear. I have confidence in you both."

Leo and Isabel left Charleston at seven o'clock the following morning. It was over five hundred miles to Washington and they were going to do it in one day. It was raining.

Leo said very little as they got onto 95 and started the long drive north. He was driving and his concentration on the road was an almost tangible thing. Isabel leaned back in her seat, eyes half-closed, and drowsed.

"We're going to be even later than I thought," he said after about an hour. "Unless the rain lets up, that is."

Isabel sat up straighter. "We'll drive it in two-hour shifts—that's the safest way. I was very careful to stop every couple of hours on the way down."

"You sound like an advertisement for Triple A."

Isabel shrugged. "I don't do that much driving

because a car is only a nuisance in New York. So I suppose I err on the side of caution."

He rubbed his head. Even in this gloomy weather his hair looked bright. "I'm sorry, Isabel. Rainy mornings don't bring out the best in me."

She half-smiled. "That's all right."

They drove for perhaps another ten miles. Then Leo said, "Who is Bob?"

Ah ha, thought Isabel. I knew it was coming.

"Bob is the fellow I share an apartment with," she replied calmly. She had answered that same question for the last three years in the same tone.

"I see. He's an architecht?"

"Yes. We were at Cooper Union together. He's enormously talented."

"You've been together since college, then?"

"I moved in with him after my father died," Isabel said shortly.

Leo nodded, put on his blinker, and moved into the left lane. Once he was around the large moving van that had been disturbing him, he turned to glance at Isabel. "If you want to give me orders to shut up, I will," he said. "I just realized I must sound like the Grand Inquisitor."

The easy smile, the gentle drawl, disarmed her. "I don't want to give you orders," she said, "but I guess I am a little sensitive about my private life. The modern urge to public confession seems to have passed me by completely."

"Is there a lot of public confession in New York?" he asked curiously.

"Psychotherapy has a good deal to answer for, as far as I'm concerned," Isabel said firmly. "There's a lot to be said for the old-fashioned virtues of reserve and self-discipline."

Someone abruptly pulled into the lane in front of him and Leo tooted his horn in admonition.

"You'll like Washington, then," he said. "It's a very reserved city, very formal. The mere thought of letting it all hang out would fill any good Washingtonian with horror."

"That does sound nice." Isabel smiled ruefully. "When I think of the number of times I have been forced to listen to the whole sad story of someone's life, I could weep."

"No one talks about their personal lives in Washington. They talk politics."

"That will make for a nice change," said Isabel.

"Are you interested in politics, Isabel?"

"My dear Senator"—she turned to regard his profile—"I'm Irish. When I was ten years old, I was reading the editorial page of *The New York Times* so I'd be able to talk to my father at the dinner table."

"You'll have to switch to the *Washington Post* for a while."

Isabel curled her legs under her and turned in her seat to see him better. "Do they really talk politics all the time?"

"Pretty much. It's inevitable, I reckon."

"Because that's what most everyone is involved in?"

"Not really. One presumes that a group of bankers would have something else to talk about besides banking. It's the very nature of the kind of entertainment Washington excels in: the formal dinner party. Imagine, there you are, seated between two women whom you scarcely know, and you must spend the first half of the meal talking to the lady on your right and the second half to the lady on your left though you may not have a thing in common with either of them. In other cities this could be very awkward, but in Washington you can always fall back on politics."

"Good heavens," said Isabel. "It sounds rather daunting."

"It can be, I reckon, but I love it. You can't get away with a sloppy thought or an undocumented fact, you know, not even in casual dinner conversation. Someone will infallibly pick you up on it."

"You are terrifying me."

"Am I?" He glanced her way, a quick flash of blue before his eyes went back to the road. "You should be able to handle it. I was in the library yesterday and I looked up Cooper Union. You didn't get in there on just your looks."

"I was lucky," she answered. "Like you."

"Mmm. Did your father ever get involved in politics, or was he an armchair critic?"

Isabel then astonished herself. "For the last ten years of his life my father did nothing but drink. The only reason he held down his job at the end was because his friends covered up for him. He didn't read anything; he just sat at the bar all night." The bitterness in her voice was audible even to her own ears. She bit her lip. "Sorry, that was unnecessary. And after all I just said about public confessions."

"I'm the one whose sorry, honey," he said gently. "You interest me and so I've been houndin' you with questions. I didn't mean to rub an unhealed wound."

Isabel bent her head. "It is an unhealed wound, I suppose. I used to love him so much, and then he went and did that to himself. I can't forgive him. I don't think I ever will."

Leo glanced once more at her, at the fine narrow head bent over the tensely clasped hands in her lap. She was taut with stillness, a controlled, intense stillness.

"Did he begin to drink after your mother died?" he asked softly.

She nodded mutely and Leo felt a sudden surge of tenderness and pity sweep through him. Poor kid, he thought, she had lost both her parents in one fell swoop.

"There's nothing I can say that I'm sure you haven't heard before," he said after a minute. "Except that if you can't forgive him, you really must try to forgive yourself."

Her head lifted at his comment. There was such a deep and lonely watchfulness about her, he thought.

"Do you think so?" Her voice sounded odd, breathless.

He nodded gravely. "You didn't fail him. In a case like his, there is quite literally nothing one can do. He had to do it for himself."

"That's what Bob says too," Isabel mumbled.

"Bob is right," Leo replied evenly. "The failure was your father's, and it was a failure of self-discipline, of hope, of loving you enough." Leo heard Isabel's forcible intake of breath as he said the last words.

"You ought to go into the psychotherapy business yourself," she said shakily. "You're damn good at it."

He shrugged, his big shoulders moving easily under the tan sweater he was wearing. Isabel was keenly aware of his physical presence, and the feeling was oddly comforting.

"When I was in college, I worked in the Big Brother program. The boy I was a Big Brother to came from a broken home—his father was an alcoholic."

Isabel was silent as she listened to the sound of the rain teeming on the car's roof. "I see. So you have some firsthand experience."

"I've seen the havoc that particular illness can wreak on a family, at any rate." He leaned forward to adjust the defroster. "But Jimmy came through it all right. He was a very self-reliant kid—like you. He's at Notre Dame right now." He grinned. "In fact, in the last letter I had from him he told me he had rejoined the Big Brother program, this time on the other end."

"You still keep in touch with him?"

"Sure. He's a great kid. A wonderful musician."

"Not a football player, then?"

"No. He came once to a Notre Dame game. I think he felt he owed it to me. He was very polite, told me it was 'interesting.' "

"Is Notre Dame the best college for a boy like that?"

"Probably not." He put on his blinker and began to pull off into a roadside gas station and cafeteria. "He should be at a good music school, really. But he didn't want to be too far from his mother. He's her only child and she isn't well." He stopped the car and turned to her. "Let's get a cup of coffee and then you can take over the wheel."

"Fair enough. Do you by any chance have an umbrella?"

"I do not. On the count of three, we run for it. One—two—three." The car door slammed and they both dashed, laughing, through the heavy rain to the restaurant door.

Chapter Five

❧

They didn't arrive in Washington until almost midnight. Leo had driven the last five hours. Isabel, exhausted, was only dimly aware of a street lined with trim Federal-style houses as Leo ushered her into the entrance hall of one of them.

"How nice," she said feebly, looking around her and blinking in the suddenly soft light.

He grinned. "You're groggy. I'll give you the tour tomorrow." He lifted her suitcase and tote bag. "Come on, I'll show you up to your bedroom."

"My paints . . ."

"I'll get them out of the car, don't worry. Come 'long now and stop arguing."

Isabel laughed and moved toward the stairs. "I can see you had generals for ancestors."

"Blood will tell," he said from behind her. "Second door on the left."

Her bedroom was very similar in style to the one she had occupied in Charleston. The Sinclairs, she reflected a little wryly, seemed to be lousy with eighteenth-century furniture.

Leo put her suitcase down in front of an elegant mahogany highboy. "The bathroom is here," he said as he opened a door and showed Isabel an incongruously modern facility. "The bed should be made up, I called Mrs. Edwards yesterday to tell her a guest was coming with me." He twitched the spread back and ascertained that there were indeed sheets and blankets on the four-poster. Then he looked at Isabel.

"All right?" he asked. "Is there anything else you need?"

She shook her head. "No. Thank you, Leo. Everything is lovely."

"Sleep well," he said, and left the room, closing the door softly behind him.

Isabel fished her pajamas and toothbrush out of her suitcase, spent three minutes in the bathroom, crawled into bed, and went immediately to sleep.

The next morning she awoke to sunshine streaming in through the window. After a few lazy minutes in bed, Isabel went into the bathroom, surveyed the modern shower and ample supply of fluffy towels, and quickly got her shampoo from her bag. She finished waking up under a refreshing spray of hot water.

Half an hour later she went downstairs and peered around for some signs of life.

"In here, Isabel," came Leo's unmistakable voice, and she went through the very elegant and formal dining room to what she supposed would be called a breakfast room. Leo was seated at a painted pine table with a plate of scrambled eggs in front of him. He stood up and smiled at her as she came in. Paige had told Isabel that her brother's slow, lazy, blue-eyed smile had broken half the female hearts in America. Isabel was quite certain Paige had not exaggerated.

"Good morning," he drawled. "Sleep well?"

"Good morning," she replied crisply, neglecting to mimic his accent. "Yes, thank you, I slept very well. I was exhausted, though I don't know why. You did the lion's share of the driving."

"It was a long day," he said. "Sit down."

He gestured to the chair next to his, and as Isabel complied, he called over the half-wall that separated the breakfast room from the kitchen, "Are there any more eggs, Mrs. Edwards?"

A heavyset black woman came over to the wall opening. "There sure are, Senator." Her accent was unmistakably Caribbean. "Good morning, miss. What can I get you?"

"Scrambled eggs will be fine," said Isabel, as she picked up the coffeepot and poured herself a cup. "I'd like to make a start on the portrait this morning, if that's all right with you," she said as she stirred cream and sugar into her coffee.

"All right," he said calmly. "I reckon I can give you three hours every morning—from seven-thirty to ten-thirty. Will that be all right?"

It would have to be. "Fine," she said. She fixed level brown eyes on his face. "But you must be prompt," she said sternly.

"Yes, ma'am," he drawled, and her face broke into a smile.

After breakfast Isabel set up her easel in the library, a beautifully wainscoted, book-lined room that had big windows facing the east. The early-morning light was marvelous.

Isabel suggested poses for Leo, but ultimately decided he should simply stand in front of a wall of old, leather-bound books, with the light from the window illuminating his face clearly against the muted background of browns and deep reds and greens. She gave him a book to hold in his hand and turned him so that he would be looking toward her, his face slightly tilted. It was a distinctly old-fashioned pose that Isabel thought would please Mrs. Sinclair.

Leo was not a problem subject. Isabel had never worked with a nonprofessional model who was as relaxed and unself-conscious as he. And it wasn't just that he was accustomed to performing in front of thousands of people, either. There was something about him, a serenity she thought had always been a part of his nature; a beautiful ease that came from always being certain of oneself and of one's position in the world. He was a "patrician." That word had always left a bad taste in Isabel's mouth, she associated it with snobbery and insensitivity to the needs of others. She associated it with Marie Antoinette and let-them-eat-cake. But this time it did not leave a bad taste in her mouth at all.

In fact, it was the quality about him that she was most concerned to catch in her portrait. He was beautiful, certainly. She was painting him in the V-neck sweater his mother had suggested, his pin-striped shirt opened at his throat. The morning light played mercilessly on the strong bones of his face, on the thick gilt hair, and on the brilliant blue of his eyes. But it was not just his beauty that made him so striking. Nor was it the unmistakably masculine magnetism that Isabel admitted was there as well. It was a certain fortunate, brilliant, exceptional look—the look of a man of happy temperament and high civilization. It was that look, more than anything else, that provoked one to wish oneself, almost blindly, in his place. Isabel found herself hungering to get her brush in hand. There were hundreds of good-looking, sexy men in the world, she thought, and she had no desire to paint any of them. But Leo . . . Leo was a rarity. She had known that, instinctively, when she had first met him. He had something his brother, for instance, who was very like him physically, did not have. It was that something Isabel's fingers ached to catch on canvas.

After Leo left for his office, Isabel worked for another hour and finally cleaned her brushes. Then she looked around the house.

Compared to the Sinclair's Charleston home, Leo's house on Q Street was modest. Isabel, however, didn't have any illusions about its being modest in price. Georgetown was the supremely desirable area for Washington urban dwellers, the most popular place to live for permanent government-oriented people with a taste for the capital's social life. Real estate in Georgetown was probably through the roof, she thought as she peered out into the walled garden at the back of the house.

"I'm just not an apartment or hotel person," Leo had told her that morning during their first sitting. "The thing I hated most about my years in football were all those hotels I stayed in while on the road."

"Did you have a house in Dallas?" she asked, staring intently at the line of his shoulders.

"No. I had an apartment. I hated it. I went home to Charleston every chance I could get."

Isabel began to paint. "I've never lived anywhere

but an apartment. It depends on what you're used to, I guess."

"I reckon."

"You're used to eighteenth-century furniture and Oriental rugs, so naturally you would find a modern apartment uncomfortable."

"Let 'em eat cake," he drawled, and startled, Isabel's hand stilled and she stared at his face.

Then, after a brief pause, she grinned. "*Vive la revolution,*" she retorted.

"*Vive la revolution,*" he repeated amiably. "The Sinclairs were poor as church mice for a century or so, you know. We lost our plantation in the war—the Yankees burned it. All that was left was the Charleston house and the furniture. It was pretty threadbare by the time my father inherited it."

"So it was your father who recouped the family fortune, then."

"Yes." He grinned. "By selling property to rich Yankees who wanted some sun. Poetic justice, I call it."

Isabel chuckled. "Poetic justice it is." She tilted her head a little to one side. "Can you raise your chin just a trifle, Leo? That's it. Good." She resumed her painting, and after twenty more minutes Leo had left for his office in the Senate Office Building near the Capital.

But that conversation had made clear to Isabel why a bachelor would bother to buy a house like this rather than stay at the Watergate or the Mayflower Hotel. Leo wasn't a transient sort of person, she thought as she collected the map he had given her and prepared to investigate the city. That was one of the things that made him different from the vast majority of modern Americans. He was a man with roots who still called Charleston home.

Leo arrived home at five-thirty, took his jacket off, and relaxed comfortably in the casual sitting room which held the television and the newspapers and the bar. Isabel had been watching the news on TV when he joined her. He fixed himself a drink and Isabel a ginger ale before sitting on the sofa with her. He loosened his tie and leaned his head back against the cushions.

"I had a desk full of reports to get through," he said after a minute. He took a sip of his drink. "I had to bring a few home with me."

Isabel didn't understand why she should feel so strange with him, but she did. She felt as if her skin were suddenly too thin, as if she could feel his every movement and change of expression in all the exposed nerves of her body. She sat up straighter. "What sort of 'repawts,'" she drawled, hoping to disguise her unsettled feelings by falling back on familiar territory.

He wasn't even looking at her; his eyes were on the television. Isabel stared, fascinated, at his relaxed figure beside her. Leaning back, his drink held between his long, strong fingers, his long legs stretched out on the Oriental rug, he answered absently "Committee reports, mainly." His eyes were still on the television anchorman.

Isabel turned her own attention to the TV and tried to watch the show as well, but when it was over, she couldn't have repeated a word the smoothly spoken, good-looking newsman had said.

Leo turned to her with a smile. "I thought we'd

eat out at a restaurant tonight," he said. "Just the two of us. Tomorrow we go to dinner at the Stacks." He took a last swallow of his drink and Isabel saw the muscles in his throat move.

There was a moment's blank pause and then Isabel's eyes widened.

"The Hamilton Stacks?" she squeaked.

His blue eyes were full of amusement. "The Hamilton Stacks."

"Hamilton Stack, the former Secretary of State?"

"The same."

"My, my, my," she said then. "You do fly in high circles."

His eyes narrowed just slightly. "It's my famous Southern charm."

Isabel's dark eyes regarded him thoughtfully and then, all of a sudden, it was as if a shutter came down over her face. "It must be very wearing, such popularity." Her tone was slightly caustic.

He put his drink down and stretched. His muscles were obvious even under the tailored fabric of his white dress shirt. He looked a little bewildered by her sudden change of tone. "I manage," he said amiably.

Isabel looked at him from behind a screen of composed reserve. She stood up. "What time do you want to leave?" she asked.

"I have a reservation for seven-thirty."

"I'll go change."

She left the room unhurriedly and went up the stairs to her room, but her thoughts weren't nearly as calm as her outward demeanor. She had suddenly realized what was the matter with her: she was falling victim to that famous Southern charm.

"Damn," said Isabel out loud as she closed the door of her bedroom behind her. "Damn and blast." She went over to the closet and opened it. "Half the females in America . . ." she muttered. "Well, not this one, Senator. Forewarned is forearmed. I am here to paint your portrait. And that is *all*."

Chapter Six

They went to the Sans Souci restaurant for dinner.
Isabel was distantly pleasant in the car. Leo was
serenely courteous. When they walked into the restaurant, Isabel noticed a distinct sway of heads
turning in their direction. The heads moved with
them as the maître d' escorted them across the floor
to one of the booths under the rear balcony.

"I've never been out with a celebrity before," she
remarked coolly as she slid into her seat.

Leo gave a wine order to the waiter, and when
the man had left, he looked gravely over the table at
Isabel. The dim table lamp underlit his hair and his
eyes and his cheekbones.

"People look at you all the time," he said quietly.
"You should be accustomed to it by now."

His remark startled her, and her dark eyes widened. "People don't stare at *me!*"

An odd expression, half-understanding, half-
rueful, rested for a moment on Leo's face. "Haven't
you noticed?" he asked gently.

Isabel's eyes held his blue gaze for a moment and
then dropped to regard the salt and pepper shak-
ers with great intensity. "It's you they were looking
at," she said.

There was a moment's silence. Then, astonishingly and seemingly utterly at random, he said, "Some man sure did a job on you, didn't he?"

Isabel felt as if the bottom had dropped out of her stomach. Her head jerked upward, color flamed in her cheeks. "How did you know . . ." she began, and then broke off. His blue eyes were full of sympathy and tenderness. Southern charm, she thought abruptly. She brushed a nonexistent strand of hair away from her temple and said, hardly, "Do you do this sort of thing for your own private entertainment?"

There was a flicker of some emotion in his eyes, but his voice, when he answered, was undisturbed. "What do you think?"

She stared at him, half in hostility and half in uncertainty. She forgot that they were in a restaurant, forgot everything but the look in that steady blue gaze. Then someone passed by their table and stopped to say something to Leo. His attention was distracted as he spoke to the man courteously, although a thin line appeared between his brows. The conversation was brief, but it gave Isabel a chance to collect her composure. When he turned back to her, she gave him an impersonal smile and said, "I'm hungry. Shall we order?"

"All right," he answered after a moment. "I think I'm in the mood for fish tonight. What about you?"

They ordered, and when the salad had been brought, he began to talk about one of the reports he had found waiting for him that afternoon. It wasn't long before Isabel was absorbed in what he was saying. By the time coffee was served, she was sitting with her elbows on the table, relaxed, unself-conscious, discussing the merits of a particular bill that was to come before Leo's committee that week as if it were the most natural thing in the world.

Leo looked with understanding at the young face across the table from him.

"Do you want some more coffee?" he asked.

"No, thank you."

Leo glanced up and their waiter approached instantly.

"Check please."

"Certainly, Senator."

Then Leo and Isabel were in his car and driving through the quiet Washington streets.

"Would you like to come for lunch in the Senate dining room tomorrow?" he asked after a few minutes.

"I'd love that." She grinned and said, "Bob is going to be green with envy when I get home."

"I just hope he's not green with jealousy," Leo returned easily. "He wasn't upset that you were staying with me?"

"Of course not." There was a pause and then Isabel said, a little gruffly, "We don't have that sort of a relationship."

Neither of them said anything else until Leo stopped the car in the narrow driveway next to his house. Then he turned to her, slid a little way across the seat in her direction, and with perfect and natural authority took her in his arms and bent his head to kiss her.

Isabel was stunned—so stunned that she was quiet in his embrace for several long seconds. His kiss was gentle, not demanding, and she had a sudden, overwhelming desire to nestle into his arms, to close her eyes and let him hold her, kiss her, love her. It was her own impulse more than his embrace that made her stiffen against him. He released her immediately.

"That is not professional behavior at all," she said, and hoped he didn't notice that her breathing wasn't quite under control.

He didn't answer and she opened the car door and walked steadily to the front door of the house. Unfortunately it was locked and she had to wait for him to come and let her in.

Leo turned the key in the lock and quietly opened the door. She was agonizingly aware of his closeness, of his size, of his hair shining like gilt in the glow of the doorstep lamp. She carefully avoided brushing against him as she walked into the front hall.

"I've never raped anyone in my life," he said humorously, "and I promise not to start with you."

Suddenly, humiliatingly, Isabel felt tears stinging her eyes. "Hell," she said violently, and she turned to run up the stairs.

A strong arm reached out and circled her shoulders and she found herself being walked steadily down the hallway and into the sitting room.

"You're not going to run away," Leo's voice said above her head. "You've been running away for long enough, I think." He put his hands on her shoulders and made her sit down on the sofa.

"What do you know about it?" she said shakily. A drop fell from her eyes onto her clenched hands. "I'm not a candidate for a Big Brother," she added, and disregarding the tears she could no longer hide, she stared up at him defiantly.

He sat down beside her. "I know. You already have a big brother, I think. Isn't that what Bob is?" He put his hand into his pocket and handed her his hankerchief.

Isabel took it, dried her cheeks, and blew her nose. "You don't do much crying, do you?" he asked noncommittally.

She laughed a little unsteadily. "The last time I cried was the day I graduated from Cooper Union. I came home to find we had been evicted from our apartment—Daddy had neglected to pay the rent."

Thank God he didn't offer her pity. The one thing she did not want was pity. "Surely you had learned by then not to trust him with paying the bills," Leo said.

"Of course I had." A strand of black hair had come down from her chignon and lay coiled like silk on her shoulder. "The end of the term was frantically busy, though. I put the exact amount of money into an addressed envelope and told him to get a money order on his lunch hour and mail it. He didn't drink in the morning. And he told me he had bought the money orders. I did that for four months and then came home and found all our belongings out on the street."

Leo sighed. "That's an alcoholic for you."

For some strange reason, she began to feel better. "I suppose so."

"Drugs are the same. I knew a few fellows who were on cocaine." He shrugged. "You lose them. There's nothing left: no dignity, no honesty, no love. Nothing. Just the drug."

"But why, Leo? Why would someone do that to himself?"

He grinned crookedly. "Honey, if I could answer that question, I'd be more famous than Freud."

She gave him a shadowy smile. "I guess you would be." She turned her head then and stared straight ahead, at the blank television set.

"You were right about Bob," she said quietly. "He has been a big brother to me. I would never have been able to get as far as I have as a painter if it wasn't for him." She seemed to realize for the first time that her hair had loosened, and she raised her hands to try to push it up again. He watched the deft movements of her fingers, her sternly beautiful profile. She bent her head a little forward and then raised it again. Her neck was long, slender, and delicate, and the line of her breasts under the fine wool dress was emphasized by the movement of her arms. Some of the peacefulness left Leo's face as he studied her.

"I could never have afforded to live on just my salary," she continued. "When Daddy died, I would have had to get a second job, but Bob let me move in with him. He pays the rent and the utilities. I just buy the food." She raised her hand once more to smooth back her hair. "There are two bedrooms," she added a little awkwardly.

"I see. So you have financial security and time to paint. What does Bob get out of this arrangement?"

"He gets his meals cooked, his house cleaned, and his laundry done," Isabel said tartly.

"I see." Leo stretched his legs out in front of him. "Does he also get a little professional camouflage?"

Isabel's mouth dropped open. She stared at him. "How did you know?"

"Isabel, honey, there is no way in this world that a heterosexual man could live with you for three years on the terms you have just described to me."

Isabel closed her mouth. "Oh."

"I believe you said he works for a very stuffy architectural firm?"

"Yes. They think our living together is racy and modern and slightly scandalous. I get speeches at every dinner about how I should let him marry me. But they would not accept the truth at all—or at least Bob doesn't think they would."

"What do you think?"

"I don't think they'd want to lose Bob, whatever his sexual preference may be. He's tremendously talented. And he's a super guy. Everyone likes him because it's impossible not to like him." She turned her face back to the empty television. "He's been an absolute Rock of Gibraltar for me," she said flatly.

"Yes," said Leo very quietly, "it rather sounds as if he has been."

Her gravely thin face suddenly broke into its wonderful smile. "I'm glad you said that. Not everyone would understand."

"I reckon not."

She tilted her head a little to one side and regarded him curiously. "Frankly, I'm rather surprised to find you so tolerant."

"Because I'm a big macho football player?"

His face was expressionless, but Isabel understood, with great surprise, that she had hurt his feelings. Impulsively she put out her hand and covered his. "Leo, I'm sorry. I'm as bad as the people who would condemn Bob."

He looked for a minute at their two hands lying on his thigh. Isabel's narrow palm was about half the size of his. Her gaze followed his and she laughed a little nervously. "My skin is about three shades darker than yours," she said as she removed her hand.

"You have beautiful coloring." His gentle, slow, Southern voice sounded like a caress.

"You're the one with the spectacular coloring," she retorted quickly. "And it's my job to catch it on canvas. And, if we're going to start at seven-thirty tomorrow morning, I had better turn in."

He smiled at her, slow and charming and utterly seductive. His eyes were even bluer than usual. "All right," he drawled. "You go on up to bed. I'm going to stay here and watch the news."

Isabel realized, with terrified astonishment, that she didn't want to leave him.

"Good night," she said firmly, and walked out of the room, feeling suddenly empty.

She did not go to sleep right away, but lay awake, consciously thinking about the portrait, about what she was going to work on tomorrow, about anything that might distract her from the upheaval of her emotions.

After a while she heard Leo come upstairs. His footsteps came along the hall and moved unhesitatingly past her door. He walked lightly for so big a man. He was like a giant cat, she thought, a giant golden cat. She opened her eyes and stared into the dimness of her room. Damn, she thought. Damn,

damn, damn. He got to her as no one had in a long time. Not since Philip.

Philip. She closed her eyes and for the first time in years she tried to visualize his face. It wouldn't come clear for her. She remembered his curly black hair and blue-gray eyes, but she couldn't remember his mouth. She couldn't really remember his face.

Now, wasn't that funny? she thought. She couldn't remember what Philip looked like. She had been so sure his face would be engraved on her soul for the rest of her life.

He had been teaching an evening art class on the Italian Renaissance at the Metropolitan Museum when Isabel met him. He was thirty years old, very handsome, a painter whose work was exhibited in the best New York galleries. Isabel had listened to him in wide-eyed wonder, thirsty for the knowledge he was imparting, awed by the looks, the intelligence, the talent of the man in front of her. When he had spoken casually to her after the third class, she had been thrilled. After the next class he had invited her out for coffee. It had not taken him very long to get her into bed.

Isabel thought that he was wonderful and that she was in love with him. She was very young and very alone and very vulnerable. She was overwhelmed by the thought that such a brilliant, handsome, successful, talented man could possibly be interested in her. She did not know that he was married.

She found it out, brutally, when she went to one of Philip's exhibitions. She had come into the Fifty-seventh Street gallery dressed in her jeans and sweater, but she hadn't minded the fact that she had no other clothes to wear. In fact, she was scarcely aware of all the well-dressed people around her. She was even less aware that the attention she attracted was not due to her casual clothes. Isabel was aware only of the paintings and of the man who was standing among a small group of people in the corner of the gallery. She didn't go over to him but began instead to look at his work.

Philip was an Abstract Expressionist. Isabel's classes in high school were mainly drawing classes; everything she knew about nonrepresentational art she had learned from Philip. So, as she looked attentively at the paintings in front of her, the expression on her young face was gravely intent.

"Isabel." It was Philip's voice, and she turned to him, a smile illuminating her darkly serious face.

"Hello, Philip," she said simply. It was a minute before she noticed the mink-coated woman standing next to him. Then he introduced her to his wife.

Even at seventeen, Isabel had learned to guard her expression. She had managed to get through the next half-hour with at least a semblance of poise. When she had finally reached home, she had been too shocked to even cry.

Philip waited after school for her the next day, and over coffee he was charming, apologetic, regretful, but firm. Maureen was from one of the best New York families, and it was her money that allowed him to paint, her connections that had gotten him his first exhibition. He had no intention of breaking up such a lucrative union, though none of this, of course, interfered at all with his feelings for Isabel.

Isabel had left the coffee shop, gone home, and refused to see him again. He had telephoned her and waited after school for her, but in the end he had given up and left her alone.

Isabel had never even kissed a man since.

Until tonight.

"Some man sure did a job on you," Leo had said to her, and Isabel still didn't understand how he had known that. She did understand that he was the first man since Philip and her father who had been able to make her cry. She also understood that if she wanted to maintain her peace of mind, she had better keep away from him. How the hell was she going to be able to keep away from him when she was living in the same house with him? When she was painting his bloody portrait, for God's sake?

It was a question she still had not resolved when she finally fell asleep.

Chapter Seven

The following day, Friday, Isabel painted during the morning and had lunch with Leo in the Senate dining room. She spent all of the afternoon at the National Gallery of Art and came home to find her dresses from New York along with a cherry-colored wool suit Bob had "picked up," he wrote, "in Lord and Taylor's on sale." It was size eight and fit her perfectly. Bless Bob, thought Isabel, who had worn her burgundy paisley for lunch with Leo and had thus, in two days, exhausted her repertoire of daytime dresses. The suit would be a welcome addition to her limited wardrobe.

Leo was home in time to have a drink and watch the six-o'clock news. Isabel curled up comfortably in her corner of the sofa with a ginger ale and thought that this was quite a pleasant ritual they shared. They talked very little and Leo sipped his Scotch slowly. It was his time to relax and unwind, Isabel realized, and she was content to sit quietly beside him on the comfortable sofa.

When the news was over, he switched the television off and turned to Isabel with a smile. "Well, are you ready to make your first foray into the wilds of social Washington?"

Isabel wrinkled her nose. "I'm petrified," she confessed.

"You needn't be." He was quite serious now. "A lot of people think the Stacks are a bunch of stuffed shirts, but it isn't true. They're very formal, but also very kind. I think you'll like them."

Isabel got lithely to her feet. "The question," she said austerely, "is will they like me?"

"They love beautiful, stuck-up young painters," he said.

Isabel stared. "Stuck-up?" she said finally, when she had gotten her breath back.

"The question," he said with a fair imitation of the reserved manner she had meticulously maintained with him all day long, "the question is, Are you stuck-up or are you scared?"

Isabel's stare turned to a glare. "Leo Sinclair, will you please stop psychoanalyzing me?"

"Scared, I reckon," he said.

"I am trying to maintain a professional relationship with you," Isabel began calmly and carefully, "but you are going out of your way to make it difficult for me."

He smiled at her, very blond and blue in the light of the table lamp. "I am," he admitted.

"Well, stop it." She tried to look and sound severe, but the sight of him in the lamplight was doing strange things to her insides.

"You have one hour to get dressed," he said softly.

"Oh." Isabel hesitated, looked at him once more, and then turned and went up the stairs to her room.

She put on one of the dresses she and Mrs.

Sinclair had bought: a designer dinner dress with an ivory satin, side-draped top and a slim ivory velvet skirt. It had been out of season in Charleston and so she had gotten a good price on it. The neck was high, so she did not need a necklace. She wore long drop earrings and did her hair in a simple, elegant chignon.

Leo was waiting for her as she came down the stairs, and she caught a glimpse of their reflection in the tall narrow hall mirror. With an artist's detachment she realized that they made a striking couple, he so tall and strong and blond, she tall but slim and dark. They were opposites, she thought as she drew a shawl around her shoulders and preceded him out the door. There could be no middle ground between the rich aristocratic Southern senator Leo Sinclair and the lower-middle-class young painter from New York that was herself.

The Stacks house was in a section of Washington that Leo called Kalorama. The homes were much larger than those Isabel had seen in Georgetown.

"That's the French embassy there," Leo said casually as they passed the imposing edifice.

The house they dined at was scarcely smaller than the embassy. As they entered through the front door, Isabel looked around and thought that the hall of the Stack house was wider than the entire width of Leo's Georgetown home.

They surrendered their outer wraps to a butler and proceeded past a huge vase of flowers and up a staircase to an enormous drawing room. This room was empty and Leo put his hand under Isabel's arm and guided her across a huge amount of thickly carpeted space to another drawing room, where, finally, there was a gathering of people.

Mr. and Mrs. Stack immediately greeted Leo and looked at Isabel with pleasant, smiling eyes.

There were a number of people already present, and right after Leo and Isabel came a succession of new arrivals. All the men were impeccably attired in black tie and the women in long dresses. Leo and Isabel were the youngest people there.

Butlers saw to it that everyone had drinks. Isabel drank ginger ale and conversed pleasantly with a variety of people, including a syndicated political columnist, a Supreme Court Justice, and a lady who ran an exclusive Georgetown boutique. Trays of canapés were circulated by other butlers and uniformed maids. Isabel was starving and crunched away on raw cauliflower and a fluff of hot pastry.

Promptly at nine o'clock guests started moving toward the dining room. Isabel obediently followed the crowd back across the second empty drawing room and into a large and elegant dining room set with two rectangular tables. Each table seated ten, and Isabel found her own place card was not at Leo's table. She panicked for a moment when she realized that he was not going to be sitting next to her and that she was going to have to get through this intimidating dinner all by herself. She allowed the man next to her to seat her and she sat gracefully, her head held high on its slim, proud neck.

The man next to her smiled pleasantly and said, "I'm Stanford Ames, the director of the National Gallery." This was said not boastfully but simply and kindly. He was merely giving her some necessary background so they could converse.

"The National Gallery," said Isabel reverently. "I spent the whole afternoon there today." Then, recollecting herself, "I'm Isabel MacCarthy."

"I know who you are," the man returned. "Ham told me earlier. So you're going to paint Leo's portrait?"

The soup was delicious and the main course, filet mignon, was superb, but Isabel paid little attention to the food. Leo, from the next table, watched her and smiled to himself a little. He had known she would enjoy Stan Ames. It was why he had asked Hamilton to invite him.

Halfway through dinner Mr. Ames smiled gently and said to Isabel, "I'm afraid it's time to talk to the lady on my other side. I've enjoyed this very much, Miss MacCarthy. You must let me give you lunch one day next week."

"That would be lovely," said Isabel.

Stanford Ames turned away and a voice from Isabel's other side said, "How are you enjoying Washington, Miss MacCarthy?"

It was so precisely timed that Isabel felt like laughing. At the next table she saw that Leo was now talking to the lady on his other side. Isabel grinned mischievously at the Washington investment banker who was her new conversational partner, "I'm enjoying it very much, Mr. Hawkins," she said. "Is it our turn to talk now?"

He smiled back delightedly. "It's our turn. Now tell me, what are you doing with yourself besides painting Leo's portrait?"

Thus the evening ran until they left at eleven-fifteen, when the party broke up.

"That was an early evening," Isabel commented as they got into Leo's car.

"All Washington dinner parties end early. You arrive at eight and leave shortly after eleven. It's tradition."

"The executives in Bob's firm are all as old as the people were tonight," Isabel said innocently, "and their parties don't break up until after one at least."

Leo grinned. It was too dark for her to see his face, but she could hear the smile in his voice.

"It's not their venerable years that send people home early in this town, Isabel. It's a question of status. If you hang around a party until twelve or one o'clock, people will think you don't have an important report to read before a top-level break-fast meeting at eight o'clock the next morning."

Isabel began to laugh. "Oh, my. I never thought of that." She rested her head against the back of the car seat. "Do you have a top-level breakfast meeting tomorrow?"

"Nope," he replied cheerfully. "I have an appointment to get my portrait painted in the morning and an appointment to golf with the artist in the afternoon, and then I'm going dancing with her in the evening."

"My goodness. That does sound like a busy day. And I don't golf."

"I'll give you a lesson. We'll do nine holes. It's supposed to be nice and I'd like the fresh air and exercise. This portrait painting is a very sedentary business."

"I suppose it must be," Isabel murmured. "I'm not a very physically active person myself, I'm afraid. The only exercise I usually get is walking."

"You're not into running?"

"God, no," Isabel said fervently. "Bob is. He dragged me out a couple of times. I absolutely hated it. Why did you ask?" she added curiously.

"You have the physique of a runner: light-boned and narrow, and you look to be in top physical condition."

Isabel laughed ruefully. "Heredity, not exercise. Both my parents were tall and thin." They came to a stop at a traffic light and a street lamp shone into the car. Isabel glanced at Leo out of the corner of her eye. She was not the only one who looked to be in excellent condition. Leo's shoulders might border on being massive, but his waist and hips were slim. Isabel was sure there wasn't an ounce of fat on him.

"Do you run?" she asked. Isabel had noticed that Washington appeared to be crowded with joggers, particularly at lunchtime.

"No. I usually start off the day with a swim. I'll get back to it once you've finished immortalizing me." His voice sounded perfectly normal. If Isabel hadn't been watching him, she would have noticed nothing unusual. But the light from the street lamp showed her the faintest tightening of the muscles about his mouth.

The light changed and the car started forward again. How stupid of me, Isabel thought. Of course he doesn't run. Pounding along on a hard pavement would be the worst thing possible for his knees. Swimming, on the other hand, would give him exercise without the wear and tear.

"Do you go to a club to swim?" she asked after a while.

"Yes."

"You need a house with a pool of your own," she said with an effort at lightness. "That way, you could jump in whenever it was convenient."

"One of these days I'll buy a bigger house out in McLean or Chevy Chase," he said easily. "For my present bachelor existence, however, Georgetown suits me fine."

"You've been a bachelor for a long time," Isabel said cautiously.

"I reckon I just never found a girl I wanted to marry." His slow voice took on an even more pronounced drawl than usual. "I haven't given up, though."

"Oh." She coughed. "I guess a wife would be a useful addition in Washington."

"Definitely." He sounded amused.

"She could run dinner parties for you, and so on."

"Perhaps I ought to put an advertisement in the paper." He *was* amused.

Isabel smiled into the darkness. "Wanted: one wife," she improvised. "Must be good hostess and knowledgeable about politics." She turned her head toward Leo. "Only applicants under thirty-five considered. Will that do?"

"I might run into trouble on the age requirement," he said judiciously.

"Heavens," said Isabel, "you're right. It's just the sort of thing to provoke an American Civil Liberties Union suit. We'd better take it out."

"I think so. It wouldn't do my image as an enlightened Southern Democrat any good if I were sued by the ACLU."

Isabel laughed. "Well, you'll have to hire an agency to deal with the number of applicants," she went on. "You really can't have them lining the street in front of your house."

"True. I suppose there are a number of women who would like the idea of being a senator's wife."

Isabel hadn't been thinking of his position. There would be women lining up for Leo Sinclair no matter what his job was. However, she wasn't about to tell him that. Besides, he didn't need to be told. He knew all too well the extent of his own attractiveness.

"I reckon I could give the agency a few guidelines," he continued imperturbably.

"I reckon you could," she drawled in response. Then, in her normal voice, "After all, one could hardly expect you to marry a sixty-year-old, no matter what her qualifications as a hostess."

"I'm glad you agree. Then, too, I have always preferred dark women. I reckon it comes from being surrounded by blue-eyed blonds at home all the time, but I sure do love black hair and big dark-brown eyes."

Isabel said nothing.

"And she'd have to be tall." Leo pursued his thought, seemingly oblivious to the change in atmosphere. "I get a crick in my neck talking to short women."

More silence from Isabel.

"We're home," said Leo, and he pulled into the drive and stopped the car. He opened the door on his side, and the inside car light went on. The sight of his blond head, suddenly illuminated, had a remarkable and devastating effect on Isabel. She put a not quite steady hand on her own door handle and got out of the car.

"I was coming around to open the door for you," he said gently from in front of the hood.

Isabel slammed the door behind her. "I'm a grown-up person. I can open my own doors."

He didn't reply but took her arm as they went up the front steps. Her arm was rigid in his grasp, telling him clearly that she wanted to pull away. He let her go at the top of the steps as he took the house keys from his pocket and opened the door.

Isabel walked in. "Good night," she said. "Thank you so much for taking me to the party. It was lovely, but I am tired."

He didn't make any protest, didn't attempt to touch her again. "I'm glad you enjoyed it."

She had been staring at his tie, and now, briefly, she raised her eyes to his face. His blue eyes were grave but untroubled.

"Good night Isabel," he said softly.

"Good night Leo." It was with great effort that she restrained herself from running up the stairs. Running away, he had called it last night, and he had been right. The problem was, she could run away from him, but she could not run away from herself and the feelings he stirred within her.

I like dark women, he had said. *Damn.* Hell and damn. Resolutely she curled up in bed. This man could hurt her very badly. She liked him. Aside from the potent physical response, which he must provoke in every woman he met, she liked him very much.

Isabel rolled over on her back and stared at the ceiling. He knew exactly how to make her like him, she thought. It was probably a reflex action on his part. He probably thought it was simply good manners to charm the woman he found himself in company with. If she had been a blonde he would probably have said he liked fair women.

Leo. God, she thought, but they had loved Leo tonight. In that group of high-powered government officials, Leo had been one of the lions, even though he was only a first-term senator. There was something about Leo Sinclair's character that declared you were in the presence of someone very high up in the world when you stood next to him. In fact, Isabel felt the lingering charm of Leo even as she fell softly to sleep in her comfortable bed.

They breakfasted later than usual the following morning, Saturday, and Isabel painted for a few hours, before driving to Chevy Chase to play golf.

It was a bright sunny day and the temperature was in the low sixties. Isabel wore corduroy pants and a scarlet crew-neck sweater. Leo wore khaki slacks and a pale-yellow golf jacket.

There were a goodly number of golfers on this lovely day, and Isabel felt unequipped to face the challenge.

"You play," she said to Leo. "I'll come along for the walk. I need to spend some time on a driving range or something before I attempt this."

"Don't worry about it," he said easily. "We won't hold anybody up." He grinned. "We'll probably have to let a herd of people play through while we're hunting around in the rough for your ball, but I don't mind."

Isabel looked around doubtfully. "Are you sure?"

"Yep. Come on, we'll do some practice swings first."

Isabel found it difficult to hit such a little ball. Several of her truly magnificent misses sent them both into gales of laughter, but when she did manage to connect, the ball went decently far and stayed pretty straight.

It took them four hours to play nine holes and they did let a herd of people play through, but Isabel had a marvelous time.

"That was fun," she said to Leo as they drank a couple of beers in the clubhouse after they had finished. "I've never been very keen on sports, but I liked that."

"You're not tired?"

"No. I walk miles and miles at home every day because I'd much rather walk than take the subway. That's what I liked about this." She grinned. "It's not too strenuous."

"The way you walk, honey," he retorted, "it's strenuous. I'm still puffing from trying to keep up."

"Hah," she said. "You wouldn't be puffing at the end of the decathlon. How many laps do you swim every day?"

He raised an eyebrow. "A mile."

Isabel took a sip of beer. "I knew it."

A friend approached and caught Leo's attention for a moment. Isabel politely looked out the window at the flawless lawns, but she was not thinking about the landscape.

Leo was a natural athlete, even she could see that.

It was there in the way he moved, the way he swung a club. He had been sensational as a running back, or so the magazine articles had claimed.

"Did you ever see Leo play?" a junior Cabinet official at last night's party had asked her. When Isabel shook her head, he had glanced, almost reverently, at the tall blond figure a few feet away from them.

"He was something," the man had said simply. "It was like watching a knife slice through butter, he went through a field so easily. Beautiful."

"Isabel." It was Leo's voice and she turned to find him smiling at her. "May I introduce Don Carter," he said.

"How do you do, Miss MacCarthy," the silver-haired man said. "I understand you are painting Leo's portrait."

The thought flashed through Isabel's mind that on her tombstone would be engraved the words *She Painted Leo's Portrait*. She smiled at Mr. Carter and made appropriate noises of affirmation and delight.

"Don is one of the trustees of the Corcoran Gallery of Art," Leo told her pleasantly.

"The Corcoran," Isabel repeated. "I was dying to come down last year and see your exhibit on American painting, but I never made it."

Leo waved a genial hand. "Join us for a bit, Don, why don't you?"

The distinguished gentleman seemed pleased by Leo's invitation and sat down at their table.

"If you are interested in portrait painting, you must certainly visit us," he said to Isabel. "We have one of the finest collections of eighteenth-century portraiture in the country."

Isabel was interested. "I didn't know that."

"Yes, indeed." Mr. Carter was well launched on what was obviously a favorite topic, and Isabel listened with unfeigned attention. When he left them half an hour later, it was with obvious reluctance.

Leo watched him go and then turned back to Isabel, his blue eyes glinting with amusement. "The Carters are one of the original Washington families, what they call Cave Dwellers here. Don can do you a lot of good, Isabel. He said he wanted to see your work—show it to him."

"I don't have my portfolio with me, but he can always see your portrait." She looked after Mr. Carter. "Cave Dwellers?" she echoed in bewilderment.

"Yep. This club runs to the old-guard type—you don't see that many politicals. I only got in because I'm a Sinclair of Charleston, and Charleston's old families go back much farther than Washington's do."

"Well, I'm descended from the High Kings of Tara," Isabel said sweetly.

"I've never yet met an Irishman who wasn't descended from the High Kings of Tara."

Isabel grinned. "Every Irishman is an aristocrat."

"So it seems," he said good-humoredly. He glanced at his watch. "And we had better get moving. We're to dine with the Matthewsons before going on to the dance."

"Doesn't anyone in this town ever stay home?" Isabel asked as they left the clubhouse.

"Not unless they're sick or dying." At his reply

Isabel's face broke into its sudden radiant smile, and a flicker of emotion went across Leo's serene face. In a moment it was gone. "Come on," he said. "The car is over here."

Chapter Eight

The dance that evening was given by an organization called The Dance Group. "It's simply a group of subscribers who like to get together for a dance once in a while," Leo told Isabel in the car as they drove out to McLean for the predance dinner party they had been invited to. "Being a bachelor, I don't belong, but I've been invited so many times I feel like a member. Maxine—Maxine Wallace, one of the patronesses—told me to come tonight and to bring you."

"Do you have to be accepted into this group, the way you have to be accepted into a country club?" Isabel asked.

"Yep. But it's not a big deal. The ladies in charge are all very nice." Leo spoke with the casual certainty of a man to whom doors have always been open.

The sun child, Isabel thought a little acidly. The golden boy. He had probably never had to struggle for anything in his life.

Isabel wore a plain burgundy sheath gown and no jewelry except her watch and long gold drop earrings. The jewelry on the other women seemed to point up her own lack. Well, I'm not a rich senator's wife, she thought defiantly. I'm only a poor struggling painter, thank God. And she held her dark head high, the expression on her proud young face grave and still.

She felt a little stiff at dinner; she was too aware of the jewels and the silver lamé on the other women, and too worried about the prospect of dancing with Leo. She wanted to dance with him, to feel his strong body against hers. It was this desire that worried her most of all.

The dance was held at the Federal City Club ballroom, and groups of different dinner parties converged upon the candlelit room with greetings and cheek kisses. The society orchestra played cheerful upbeat dance music, and couples spun merrily and purposefully around the floor. It was a giant party and everyone was obviously having a ball. Isabel stared. It was nothing at all like the nose-in-the-air affairs she had occasionally attended with Bob in New York.

"Well, let's give it a spin, shall we?" Leo said good-humoredly and, taking her by the hand, led her out onto the dance floor.

Leo held her in a light but firm grip and steered her effortlessly around the floor. They stopped three times to chat with other couples, and Leo exchanged greetings with at least five other people. By the end of the dance Isabel's face was bright with laughter. This was not going to be a romantic cheek-to-cheek evening at all.

"It's a good thing I took ballroom dancing in gym," she said to Leo as they left the floor. "Fox-trots are not the usual style in my group."

He chuckled. "My mama made sure I knew how

to dance. Sent me to dancing school when I was a kid." His blue eyes laughed at her. "How I hated it."

"But it's come in useful," Isabel said.

"Yep. Another case of Mama being right, as usual."

Much to her own surprise, Isabel found herself having a wonderful time. She felt less self-conscious about her dress and danced with a variety of men besides Leo, all of whom went out of their way to be nice to her. She also drank several glasses of champagne.

At twelve-thirty she was drinking her fourth glass and standing by the fountain—the courtyard had been enclosed for the occasion to serve as a bar—talking to Herbert Rand, an Associated Press correspondent. Leo was in conversation with the British ambassador just inside the ballroom, and as she listened to Mr. Rand, Isabel's eyes lingered on his distinctive blond head.

Mr. Rand followed her eyes. "He's an astonishing guy, isn't he?" he said, completely changing the subject.

"Leo?" She glanced up at the AP correspondent. "Yes," she said then. "A veritable Renaissance man."

"That's one way of putting it, certainly. He's got a brilliant future in politics, if he wants it."

"Why shouldn't he?" Isabel asked curiously.

"I don't know. It's hard to know what Leo Sinclair wants. He's a past master at seeming not to really want anything. To listen to him you'd think all of his achievements, the Rhodes scholarship, the football success, the senatorial election, just happened. You'd think he was just an easygoing guy, fortune's child, and none of it was his doing at all."

This, of course, had always been Isabel's impression of Leo. "Isn't it true?" she asked.

He glanced at her. "I know the AP sports correspondent very well. He says the last three years Sinclair played football he played in constant pain. When they finally operated, they couldn't believe he had been running on those knees." He looked over at Leo. "The last three years he played, Sinclair was All-Pro every time."

Isabel looked at Leo. "Why would he do that?" she asked.

"He loved football. And Christ, how we loved to watch him. Those damn knees. I guess he went just about as long as he could, and then some, before quitting. He was only twenty-nine. He should have had a few more years."

"I didn't know," Isabel said quietly. "I thought he hurt himself the last year he played."

"He kept quiet about it. He did it in college, actually. Bob Rossi is sure that's why he took the Rhodes; he knew he shouldn't play anymore. But I guess he couldn't stay away. It must have hurt like hell to have to quit. He had a shot at the all-time running record, you know."

"No. I didn't know."

"And now he's a senator." The AP man smiled at her. "No freshman senator has had a more royal Washington reception than Leo Sinclair. The top hostesses fall over one another to get him. He applies to clubs with ten-year waiting lists and is accepted. And through it all, there he is, Mr. Nice Guy, Mr. Easygoing." He finished his champagne.

"I understand from the aides on the Senate committees where he sits that he is, consistently, the best-prepared and best-informed senator present."

Isabel drank some of her champagne. "It would seem, then, that he is serious about politics."

"I think he is. I think he has set his sights very high indeed. Of course"—and now the correspondent looked at her with frank curiosity—"he needs a wife."

"Yes," said Isabel austerely, "I suppose he does."

"There's a huge collection of willing women, as I imagine you must know. The leading candidates at the moment are Lady Pamela Ashley, the British ambassador's daughter, and Cissy Baldwin. Cissy is divorced, however, so I think that rules her out. Sinclair is Catholic." The correspondent smiled. "But no one has seen Lady Pamela or Cissy since you arrived on the scene, Miss MacCarthy."

Isabel had never heard of Pamela or Cissy. "The senator has been very kind in introducing me around," she said warily. "He knows how helpful some Washington contacts would be to me."

"I see," said the AP man, who looked as if he saw something very different indeed.

Isabel's expression suddenly became aloof and withdrawn. "The senator's mother commissioned me," she said.

"I see," the man repeated. She could feel his eyes on her profile. Then he said very casually, "You're an extremely beautiful girl, Miss MacCarthy. You mustn't be surprised if people come to conclusions about you and the senator."

Slowly Isabel turned her head to look at the man beside her. He was struck by her stillness, her intensive, watchful stillness. "I am not beautiful and there is nothing but a professional relationship between me and the senator." Her voice was calm, even, controlled.

"I will accept the last part of your statement," the man said, his eyes on her face. "But not the first."

"Isabel." It was Leo. "They're serving some supper. Are you hungry?"

"Yes," said Isabel. No one, she instinctively knew, would say uncomfortable things to her in Leo's presence. He wouldn't allow it. It was a privilege, she reflected wryly as they went over to the buffet, that he reserved to himself.

"What were you and Rand talking about?" he asked casually as they sat down with plates of scrambled eggs and sausage.

"You," she replied.

He chewed slowly on his eggs. "Oh?"

She laughed at him. "You are the most imperturbable man I have ever known. Just *once* I would like to see you startled."

"Stick around long enough and you will," he returned amiably. He ate some sausage. "What was Rand telling you about me?"

"That you played in pain for the last three years of your football career."

A shadow of annoyance crossed Leo's face. "Don't pay any attention to him. The press is prone to exaggeration."

"Do your knees hurt you now?" Isabel persisted.

"No." His voice was unusually clipped.

"What other injuries did you collect over the years?"

He shrugged. "Nothing spectacular."

Isabel put down her fork and gave him a long dark look. "You could have crippled yourself. I suppose that thought never occurred to you?"

He put his own fork down and smiled at her faintly, his lids half hiding his very blue eyes. "It occurred to me."

"Men," said Isabel. She did not mean it as a compliment.

"I know." His voice was very gentle, almost caressing. Isabel found she could not take her eyes away from him.

"Isabel!" A rich feminine voice next to her ear made her jump. Sunny Gunther, a vivacious young woman whom Isabel had met at a previous dinner party, approached with an unknown young man. "Here is someone who is dying to meet you," Sunny said, and automatically, Isabel smiled.

The dance didn't break up until after two and both Leo and Isabel were quiet going home in the car.

"You go on up to bed," Leo said as they came in the front door. "It's late and you must be tired."

"All right." She put her hand on the stair rail and then turned to look at him. "Aren't you coming? It is, as you pointed out, very late."

"In a little while." He spoke almost absently. "I have a few things to do first."

"Oh." She felt absurdly forlorn, dismissed, and forgotten as she walked slowly up the stairs by herself.

Leo refused to sit for his portrait the following morning.

"It's Sunday, and Sunday is my day off," he told

her at breakfast. He was dressed in a well-cut light-gray suit.

Isabel said curiously, "Where are you going?"

"Church," he replied succinctly.

"Oh." She looked into her coffeecup. "I used to go when my mother was alive. I made my Communion and Confirmation. Then she died and I stopped going."

"What did your mother die from?"

Hodgkin's disease."

"I see."

"She was a wonderful person, my mother. So strong. She never complained."

There was a brief silence. "Would you like to come with me this morning?" he asked gently.

"I . . . No, I don't think so."

"All right." He didn't press her.

"I think I'll work some on the portrait's background."

"All right." He looked at his watch. "What would you like to do this afternoon when I get back?"

"You don't have to entertain me, Leo," she said firmly.

"Well, then, how about you entertaining me? I sure would like a guided tour around some art museums, conducted by a bona-fide painter."

She looked at him. "Would you?"

"I would." He smiled. "You won't believe this, but I've never been to the National Gallery."

She stared in horror. "Are you serious?"

"Perfectly."

"Well, it's time you went," she said decidedly.

"I reckon it is." He pushed back his chair and stood up. "We'll go after lunch," he said.

"God forbid you should miss a meal."

He grinned. "Honey, I have never missed a meal in my entire life. It's the rule I live by."

"I've noticed."

After he had gone, Isabel carried the dishes into the kitchen and put them in the dishwasher. Mrs. Edwards did not come in on weekends, so Isabel had made breakfast for the last two days. After a very token protest, Leo had handed the kitchen over to her with obvious relief.

As she walked toward the library, the phone rang. Isabel picked it up and said impersonally, "Senator Sinclair's residence."

"Hello, is the senator there?" It was a woman's voice and Isabel knew instantly to whom it must belong. The accent was unmistakable. "This is Pamela Ashley calling."

"I'm sorry, but the senator is at church," Isabel replied.

"I see. Would you ask him to call me when he gets in?"

"Certainly," said Isabel, and hung up the phone. The voice had sounded very sophisticated, very upper-class, very English. The British ambassador's daughter. Isabel felt unaccountably depressed as she went over to her easel and looked at the portrait she was working on. Leo's eyes looked back at her, blue and smiling and subtly authoritative. "Damn," said Isabel out loud, and then she began to mix colors.

When Leo came in from church, she told him about the phone call. He looked surprised and then immediately went to the phone in the hall. He left the library door open, and as Isabel cleaned her brushes, she unashamedly listened.

"Lady Pamela, please," he said. "This is Leo Sinclair calling." A long silence and then, "Hello, Pam. How are you?"

More silence. "I know. I've been busy." Pause. "I reckon." Another pause. "Yep. I'm being immortalized, right and proper." He laughed, a genuine rich chuckle. "I know, I know." Long silence. "I'd like to, Pam, but I promised to go to the National Gallery with Isabel this afternoon. She's going to educate me—can't believe I've never set foot in the place." Another laugh. "Yes, I know. All right, Pam. Yes. I will. 'Bye now." He hung up. Two seconds later his head appeared at the library door.

"What's for lunch?" he asked.

"You just finished breakfast two hours ago."

"I am not budging from this house until I eat."

"All right, all right. As soon as I finish cleaning up here, I'll fix you something."

"I'll go change," he informed her, and disappeared.

They had chicken salad for lunch and then went to the National Gallery. It was a wonderful afternoon. Isabel couldn't believe it when Leo looked at his watch and announced that the museum was due to close any minute.

"What a lot of bologna that was," Isabel said to him as they walked down the steps of the museum. "All that business about my educating you." Leo had proved to be a lot more knowledgeable about art than she had suspected.

"I know the periods, all right," he replied easily.

"I don't know the technique like you do. I learned something this afternoon."

She thought suddenly that he probably had. She was beginning to realize that the famous Sinclair hair covered an absolutely first-class brain. He had listened to everything she had said this afternoon, and she would bet anything that he remembered all of it.

"What kind of food would you like for dinner?" he asked as they drove homeward. "There's a nice little Italian restaurant not far from us."

"I would like to stay home," said Isabel. "I took some pork chops out of the freezer this morning. Let's have them."

"I feel a little guilty about making you cook," he confessed. "You hired on as a painter, not a chef."

"I don't mind," she said. "I like to cook. And I don't feel like having to change out of my comfortable pants and into a dress to eat out."

"I would love to eat at home," he said, "if you're sure you don't mind?"

"I don't," she said, and meant it.

Leo read the newspapers in the sitting room while Isabel worked in the kitchen. He opened a bottle of wine and they drank it with their pork chops and rice dinner. Afterward he helped her to clear the dishes and then they went back into the sitting room and watched Masterpiece Theatre on television.

At ten o'clock Leo switched the TV off and came back to sit on the sofa. He stretched his legs out in front of him comfortably.

"Would you be afraid to stay in this house by yourself until the potrait is finished?" he asked her.

Isabel's head turned with a start. "What did you say?"

"If I moved out, moved in with Stan Preston for a week, would you be afraid to stay here alone?"

She stared at him in bewilderment. "But why would you do that? What do you mean?"

He spoke almost lazily, contemplating the feet stretched so comfortably in front of him. "I mean that I am finding it something close to torture to be around you like this and not make love to you. I can't do it anymore, so I think I had better move out."

His voice was its usual slow drawl, his face held all its usual serenity. Isabel spoke uncertainly. "Are you serious?"

He turned his head and let her see his eyes. "Perfectly," he said.

Isabel's heart pounded inside her chest.

"Leo," she said. She didn't seem to have enough breath to speak and inhaled deeply. "I swore I would never get involved with a man again," she said at last.

"I know that." He didn't make a move toward her. His eyes were blindingly blue and she could read clearly in them what it was he wanted. He said, very softly, "Do you think you might change your mind and get involved with me?"

Chapter Nine

꧁

Such a simple question, Isabel thought. And one week ago it would have provoked such a simple answer. But now, she was not so sure.

She bent her head and looked at her hands clasped in her lap. A week ago, instantly, unreflectingly, she would have said no; she would have said, Go ahead, move out, leave me alone. Tonight she sat listening to the deep nocturnal silence of the house and knew she was poised on the brink of perhaps the most momentous decision of her life.

This was the man. There was something in him that reached out to her, that called to something deep in her own nature. She was suddenly quite sure that if she said no to Leo now, she would spend the rest of her life haunted by an irredeemable sense of failure and loss. Even now as she sat silently contemplating her own tensely clasped hands, she had a sense of something beginning to slip irrevocably away.

She ran her tongue across dry lips. "I'm afraid," she whispered.

"I know you are."

Her head bent farther forward. She had

guarded herself for so long the thought of throwing away all those years of safety terrified her. Leo sat at the other end of the sofa, quite motionless, and now he slowly put out his hand on the sofa between them, fingers curved upward ready to cradle hers.

"Give me your hand." It was said very gently, very softly, and she raised her eyes to his face. His hair had fallen forward over his forehead. His blue eyes were brilliant. Very slowly she unlocked her fingers and put her hand into his. Leo's hand completely engulfed hers, and Isabel shivered as he raised his other hand to touch first her cheek and then her mouth.

"Leo." It was scarcely a breath, but he heard it and suddenly moved toward her. He put an arm around her shoulder and she turned her face into his shirt. She could feel his hand on her hair, gently stroking it.

"You have such beautiful hair," he was saying. "Isabel." At the sound of her name she took her face out of his shoulder and looked up.

His kiss was not the gentle, careful kiss he had given her once before. This was something quite different, something Isabel had never known. She could lose herself in this man. She knew it, instinctively, had always known it, she realized now. She felt from the urgency of his kiss how much he wanted her, but she held back a little, frightened of letting down the defenses she had so carefully built over the years. But the flame burning in Leo was so bright. She slid her arms around his neck and let her mouth open under the pressure of his.

His hands lightly touched her narrow waist and

then one hand slid under her sweater and moved up to cup her breast. Isabel closed her eyes in pleasure, and after a minute her hand began to caress the thick bright hair at the back of his head.

"Let's go upstairs," he murmured. The touch of his hand on her breast was exquisite. Isabel opened her eyes and looked at the pale-golden hair that slipped so easily through her fingers.

"Yes," she said. "Let's go upstairs."

He rose with his distinctive fluid grace and, bending for a minute, picked her up as easily as if she had been a child. He carried her easily too, up the narrow stairs and into her bedroom, where he set her on her feet beside the bed.

"You should know this," he said to her. His hands were on her shoulders and he was standing so close that Isabel's head was tilted far back to look up into his face. "I wanted you from the first moment I set eyes on you."

Isabel's lips parted a little. "You did?"

"I did." His voice sounded normal, but she could see, above the opened collar of his shirt, a pulse beating rapidly under the lightly tanned skin. His hands slid down her shoulders to her elbows. "I do."

Isabel held the ribbed bottom of her sweater and, without saying a word, pulled it over her head. She slowly and carefully began to unbutton her shirt. Her eyes looked up at him with a dark expression veiled in mystery. His hands went automatically to the buttons of his own shirt.

Isabel watched him, almost unconscious of her own bare flesh. She had never seen him without his shirt before, and she gazed at the smoothly muscled expanse of chest, shoulders, and upper arms with an almost professional detachment. She might not be very sexually experienced, but Isabel had seen a great number of nude male bodies. Leo's was perfection. She felt a sudden, sharp regret at the thought of not painting him exactly as he was now.

Then his body bore her down onto the bed, and all thoughts of painting, or of anything else, fled from Isabel's mind. Nothing else existed in the world except Leo's hands touching her, his mouth caressing her.

Isabel had never felt like this with Philip, Philip had been interested only in satisfying himself. He had never shown her such astonishingly erotic tenderness. As Leo's hands slowly explored her body, Isabel felt passion rising in her like the spring tide until a small whimper formed deep in her throat and she arched up against him, her slender body pressing against the hard strength of his. Her long hair was streaming back against the pillow and he buried his face in it.

"Isabel." It was a love word, a caress, a promise.

She kissed his shoulder as her fingers dug into his back. She had never wanted anything in life more than she wanted him at this minute.

With Philip she had felt as if she were a spectator during their lovemaking. A part of her had always remained at a distance: detached, uninvolved, intact. With Leo she lost herself. Swept away on a tide of passion, hers as well as his, she rose to heights she had not known existed and gave to him a depth of surrender she had not dreamed possible.

And then, after the raging tide had receded and

they were left breathless, the oneness was still there. He held her in the crook of his arm and she nestled her cheek into the slightly damp hollow of his shoulder. He kissed the top of her head and she turned her lips to the smooth bare skin of his chest.

"Who was he?" he asked. His voice was slow and soft and lazy.

"His name was Philip," she said after a minute. "I was seventeen when I met him."

"I'd like to meet him." His voice was the same as before. "I'd like to beat the selfish swine into a bloody pulp!"

"Leo!" She was so startled that she sat up. "How do you know he was a selfish swine?"

His voice remained even, but the expression in his blue eyes was one she had never seen before. "I just made love to you, honey," he said. "I can tell."

She could feel the color staining her cheeks. She sat there looking down at him, her long black hair streaming down her naked shoulders and over her small, perfect breasts.

"He wasn't like you," she said.

"I should damn well think not." It was the first time she had ever heard him swear. "You were seventeen. How old was he?"

"Thirty."

This time he really swore and Isabel's eyes became utterly huge. He looked up at her and his face relaxed a little. "I'm sorry, Isabel. I shouldn't have said that."

"I've said worse," Isabel replied candidly. "It's the source, not the language, that's so shocking."

He picked up her hand and held it to his lips.

"My mama always taught me to mind my language in the presence of ladies."

"You are the complete Southern gentleman, suh," she said. Then she grinned, a mischievous urchin's grin that illuminated her grave, dark face. Her brown eyes laughed at him. He had never seen her look like this and guessed that it had been years and years since anyone had seen her look like this. "It just occurs to me that we are in rather an odd position for me to be making that comment," she said.

He felt a quick and savage anger toward the men who had taken that look from her. He moved her hand to his cheek and wrapped his free hand around a thick strand of long black hair. He pulled gently, drawing her down until her face was close to his. Then he released her and cupped her face between his hands.

"Isabel." He kissed her lips. "Honey, I wish you'd smile like that all the time." He kissed her again, with extreme tenderness. His fingers on her cheekbones were feather-light.

Isabel stopped breathing. This is happiness, she thought almost wonderingly. This is perfect happiness.

His fingers moved caressingly along her cheekbone, and very simply, as if it was something she had been doing all her life, Isabel began to kiss him. He lay still for a minute, letting her take the initiative, and then his arms came up to hold her and draw her down until her whole body was stretched on his.

She raised her head and looked down into his eyes. Passion trembled between them, and something else—something so sweet, so tender, that Isabel felt it as an ache in her throat. Her hair streamed down, enclosing their faces in a tent of heavy black silk. Even within the fall of her hair, his slightly narrowed eyes were blindingly blue. Under her his body was hard with muscle.

"Isabel," he said again very softly. "Isabel the beautiful."

"I love the way you say my name," she whispered. "No one else in the world will ever say it like you do."

At last he moved, his hands coming up to grasp her hips gently. Feeling his touch, her brown eyes widened and darkened. There would never be anything like this again. She thought that now as she felt her body ripen under his touch. She would never love anyone else like she loved him because there wasn't anyone else like him. Leo.

"Leo." She said his name aloud and moved her body against his, answering to the message his caressing hands was sending all through her. Then, more strongly, urgently, "Leo!"

Passion flared between them.

Leo rolled, and their positions were reversed with Isabel underneath him, Isabel reaching up to hold him, Isabel moving her body to accommodate his. There was fire running through her veins and a wild aching longing in her loins.

"Leo," she said. "Ah, God, Leo." She shut her eyes. She heard him saying her name, heard the love words he was using. She felt his power, and the world exploded. Without realizing it, her nails dug deeply into his shoulders. She would see the marks of them the following day.

Neither of them moved for a very long time. "I'm too heavy for you," he said finally, and rolled onto his back. Isabel turned to look at him.

"I didn't know," she said. "I didn't know it could be like that."

His profile was calm, but for a moment a smile flickered in the curve of his mouth. "Honey," he said, "that was something else."

"Was it?" She really wanted to know. "There was only Philip, you see, and it was never like that with him."

"What happened with you and Philip?" he asked. He wasn't looking at her. His eyes were half-closed and he looked as if he were going to fall asleep. Isabel was beginning to realize that he got most of his information when he looked this way.

"Is that how you operate in the Senate?" she demanded. "Do you lean back, close your eyes, put your feet up, and ask, with that oh-so-disarming drawl, 'Tell me, General, are you *sure* there isn't any fat in your budget?' "

One blue eye opened. He didn't say anything. Isabel reached over and smoothed his hair off his forehead.

"Philip was teaching an evening art course I took at the Met," she began. She had never told anyone, not even Bob, about Philip. But she told Leo. When she had finished, he was silent for a long time. She had been lying on her back, staring at the ceiling as she talked, but now she turned her head to look at him curiously.

"I'm just lying here thinking about the things I'd like to do to that fellow," he said.

"It was my own fault," said Isabel. "I was

colossally stupid, really. And do you know something? His art isn't really that good. His last exhibition got distinctly mediocre reviews."

"Do I detect a note of satisfaction, Miss Mac-Carthy?"

She went back to staring at the ceiling. "It's unworthy of me, I know, but there it is." She smiled. "My exhibition opened shortly after his. The reviews were much better."

A deep, soft chuckle sounded beside her. "I reckon you took care of him yourself, honey."

"I reckon I did." Her face sobered. "So, you see, I kept a bit of a distance between myself and men after that. I didn't need a repeat of Philip."

"No."

"Unlike you, I haven't had any experience in this sort of a situation."

"I'm not exactly Don Juan," he complained softly.

No, she thought. You're only the most beautiful man in the world, that's all. "Oh," she said. "You were perfectly innocent before I came along?"

"Isabel." He sounded amused. "I am thirty-four years old. On the other hand, I like to be able to go to Communion on Sunday. I try—let's put it that way."

"Oh." She turned to look at him. "Did you go to Communion this morning?"

He looked back at her. "No," he said, "I didn't."

"Not in the right frame of mind?" Her voice was softer than he had ever heard it.

"No." He turned on his side and reached out. "I was thinking about you." He gathered her into his arms and the curve of his body. "Go to sleep," he said. "It's late."

He was so warm, so big, so comforting. Isabel yawned. "Good night," she said, and in three minutes they both were asleep.

He wasn't there when she awoke the following morning. She looked at her clock and saw that it was after eight.

Good God. She pushed her hair back off her face and sat up. She was supposed to have started painting an hour ago.

The door opened and Leo walked in.

"Ah," he said, "good. You're awake."

"I overslept, forgot to set my alarm. Why didn't you wake me?"

He was wearing a pair of gray sweatpants and a sweatshirt. His hair looked as if it had been wet and was now beginning to dry. A few feathery gold strands had fallen across his forehead. He looked big and wide awake and energetic.

Isabel yawned. "Were you swimming?"

"Yep. I woke up at six, and since you were snoozin' so comfortably, I decided to go over to the pool." He came across the room and sat down on the edge of the bed. "I have a little time before I have to be in the office."

"Good," said Isabel. "You can sit for me for a while."

"Actually, honey"—his voice was deep, slow, caressing—"I was thinking of doing a few other things for you."

She looked up into his face. "I'm still half-asleep," she protested weakly.

He put his hands on her breasts. "I'll wake you up," he said. And he did.

Chapter Ten

Isabel had never painted as well as she painted that week.

"It will be finished in another two days, I'd say," she told Leo on Thursday.

"So soon?"

She looked at him, brush suspended in air. "You're the man who expected to be painted in four days. Remember?"

He smiled a little ruefully. "Yes, I remember."

She put her brush down and regarded her work thoughtfully.

"May I see it?" he asked.

To her knowledge, he had not looked once at the portrait since she had begun it.

"Of course." She stepped aside and he stood next to her, directly in front of the easel. He looked and Isabel looked with him.

It was, quite simply, the best thing she had ever done. It was Leo—or at any rate it was Leo as she saw him.

He was silent for so long that she became nervous. "What do you think?" she asked a little apprehensively.

His eyes remained on the picture. "I wasn't sure

how good you were," he said. "I was a little afraid."
He still did not look at her. "That's why I avoided
looking at it, I reckon."

"I see."

He turned now and looked down at her. His face
was very grave. He picked up her right hand and
stood looking at it for a long minute. "Amazing," he
said.

Suddenly she felt blindingly happy. "It's good,
isn't it?"

"It's very good." He turned back to the picture
for a minute. "Very very good."

"I'm glad, Leo. I'm so glad you like it."

He bent abruptly and kissed her, quick and hard.
"I'll get on the phone to Mama. We have a party to
give."

"You don't have to . . ."

"Not have to, want to," he replied firmly. He
glanced at his watch. "I have to change, honey. I
have an appointment with someone from the
Pentagon."

"Go ahead." She smiled at him. "I'm going to do
just a little more work here."

"Okay." He went to the library door and then
stopped and turned. "By the way, we're going to
the Messengers tonight, remember?"

They had stayed home for the last three nights.
"I remember," she said softly.

"All right. See you later, then."

"See you later."

She was absorbed in her work when he left the
house twenty minutes later.

Ron Messenger was a Washington fixture. He

had served as Secretary of the Treasury in a former administration and had also been his country's ambassador to the Netherlands a few years back. His wife was Dutch and one of the most influential of Washington's hostesses. They lived on an estate in McLean, Virginia, and an invitation to dine there was one of the most highly sought of social Washington's honors. Isabel had learned all this from Bev Breckinridge, who lived in the house next to Leo's and whose husband was a senator from one of the Midwestern states. The Breckinridges had not yet been invited to dine with the Messengers, Bev had told Isabel with some chagrin over tea the preceding day.

"Leo seems to get around," Isabel commented as she sipped her hot tea in Bev's period sitting room.

"Leo goes everywhere," Bev said. "He dines with Democrats and Republicans. He's been given an open-arms welcome by the native Washingtonians, and they usually scorn the political newcomers. Good God, he's been admitted to clubs that people who have been here for years haven't been able to breach."

"Remembeh, honey," Isabel said with a fair imitation of Leo's drawl, "he is a Sinclayeh of Charleston, not some newcomeh from New Yawk."

Bev chuckled. "True. And in many ways Washington is still a Southern city."

"And," continued Isabel in her own voice, "he tells me that as a Southern Democrat his voice is assiduously wooed by both parties."

"True again. But there are a lot of Southern Democrats in town and none of them is besieged like Leo. The thing is, everyone likes him so much."

Isabel had looked at her teacup. "He's a very likable man."

"He's a doll," Bev said warmly. "And I don't just mean his looks. He *listens* to you, really listens. He's not thinking about the person next to you or about what he's going to say when you've finished talking. He pays attention and hears what you say. Add that to the way he looks and you've got a potent combination."

"I guess so," Isabel had murmured, and changed the topic to other matters. But she thought of that conversation as she sat next to Leo on the drive out to McLean Thursday evening.

"I called Mama this afternoon," he volunteered after a little. "She's going to fly up on Wednesday. We've fixed the party for Friday. I had Miss Osborne call out invitations this afternoon.

"Oh," said Isabel. "What kind of a party did you have in mind?"

"A dinner party, with you as guest of honor. We'll hang the portrait in the drawing room for the evening. Mama says we can squeeze twenty people into the dining room.

"Oh," said Isabel again.

"I thought of having a big reception, packing the house or using the Metropolitan Club, but I think a simple dinner will do the job better. The trick is to get the people who influence the fashions, and I think I've done that. Miss Osborne had a very successful afternoon."

"Who's coming?" Isabel asked curiously. He reeled off a list of names that made her blink. "Well, there must be something I can do to help," she said after a minute.

"Not a thing," he responded cheerfully. "I had Miss Osborne book the caterers. Mama will take care of the rest."

"I see." Isabel leaned her head back against her headrest and briefly closed her eyes. When she opened them, the car had turned off the road and onto a broad driveway that wound through dense trees and opened into a wide gravel parking area in front of an imposing English manor house. A butler admitted them and steered them to a seating chart containing tiny envelopes with the names of all the guests. Isabel looked at hers and discovered she was to be taken into dinner by one of Washington's most revered columnists. She looked up at Leo.

"Who did you get?" she asked.

His face was perfectly peaceful. "Lady Pamela Ashley," he said. He took her arm and escorted her across the spacious foyer and up a few stairs into the broad drawing room where Mr. and Mrs. Messenger greeted their guests.

Isabel drank her usual glass of ginger ale and talked first to the Italian ambassador and then to one of the men she had danced with last Saturday. She smiled and listened and answered, and all the time her senses were trained on a blond head that rose several inches above the rest of the heads in the room. He was talking with an influential congressman when a stunning-looking black-haired girl came up to him and put a light hand on his sleeve. His head turned; he saw her and he smiled. Isabel knew she was looking at Lady Pamela Ashley.

Dinner had been called for eight and it was

seven-fifty when Leo brought Lady Pamela over to meet Isabel. He performed the introduction and Isabel held out her hand.

"How do you do, Lady Pamela." She spoke pleasantly, civilly, and tried not to stare at the lovely face of the British ambassador's daughter.

Pamela Ashley had hair as dark as Isabel's, but where Isabel's was heavy and straight, the Englishwoman's was feather-light and framed her face in a soft midnight dark cap of curls. Her eyes were not the arresting blue of Leo's; they were violet, almost purple, and were framed by spectacularly long black lashes. She had the flawless skin of the English, very white and smooth. She looked to be in her middle twenties.

Lady Pamela gave Isabel a cool smile and said, in her well-bred British voice, "So you are the artist who has been doing Leo's portrait." She made the word "artist" sound as if it were a glorified servant.

"Yes," said Isabel, and looked at Lady Pamela with dark and icy detachment.

"Will you be going back to New York when you have finished?" Pamela inquired.

"Possibly." said Isabel.

Lady Pamela evidently concluded that she had spent enough time addressing Isabel and turned to Leo, giving Isabel a splendid view of her shoulder. "Leo," she said, "Daddy was wondering if you would golf with him this weekend."

"I don't think so, Pam," Leo replied amiably. A pair of cobalt-blue eyes rested thoughtfully on Isabel's face. "I have to get my portrait finished up. My mother will be in town next week and we want the finished product to be ready for her."

Isabel met his eyes. She gave him back a look so intense that it seemed to scorch into his very brain, and then, suddenly, her face broke into its rare smile. "The finished product, forsooth," she said. "You make it sound like a breakfast cereal."

His lids half-closed over his eyes and he gave her back a very faint smile.

"I believe Mrs. Messenger is summoning us to dinner," said Lady Pamela.

"Miss McCarthy," said a voice behind Isabel, "I believe I am to have the pleasure of your company this evening." Isabel turned to greet the silver-haired dean of the Washington press community, and Leo offered Pamela his arm.

The stately dining room was set with one long table resplendent with flowers and silver candela-bra and princely place settings of silver, china, and crystal. Isabel looked gravely around and reflected that nothing in her previous life had prepared her for the formal splendor of social Washington.

She looked from the table to the elegant men and women seated around it. She looked at Leo, so assured and natural in this company. Why shouldn't he be assured and natural? she thought. He had been bred to this kind of a life, bred to wealth and to luxury. He was at home here, as was Lady Pamela Ashley, who had probably cut her teeth on affairs like this.

Isabel was not at home. She felt like a visitor from another planet at these dinners.

It was a feeling that had not disturbed her unduly before tonight. In fact, she had enjoyed herself a great deal. To a girl who had been brought up on stainless steel and meat loaf, all this magnificence was fun.

It was fun to be a visitor. But what would it be like, Isabel wondered, to be a part of this world permanently, to spend one's time booking caterers and arranging the flowers, to be valued for one's connections, one's social utility?

It was not for her, Isabel knew that with utter certitude. It was fun for a while, but it could never be an important part of her life, not as important as her painting.

As if on cue, her dinner partner said, "I understand you graduated from Cooper Union, Miss MacCarthy. My nephew went there a few years ago. I must say I was very impressed by it."

Isabel looked interested. "Did he? What was his name?"

It turned out that Isabel had known his nephew and they talked art schools as they spooned up jellied consommé with bits of melon on top. Arthur Stevens was known for his sharp brain and stinging political wit, but he seemed genuinely interested in Isabel's experiences in art school and in getting herself established.

After the consommé, broiled sole with toasted almonds was served and champagne was poured. Arthur Stevens began to talk about the role of the Washington press, and Isabel listened for a while and then began to ask a few telling questions. They were engaged in a concentrated discussion when the fish course was cleared and filet mignon with béarnaise sauce, pommes soufflées, and braised carrots were served. It was time to talk to the man on her other side.

"We'll finish this conversation later," Mr. Stevens promised, and Isabel turned to the congressman on her right. Leo, she was gratified to see, was no longer talking to Lady Pamela.

Isabel discussed the defense budget with the congressman, who was a cousin of Ron Messenger's and who sat on the House Defense Committee. During the dessert, an ice-cream bombe, they talked about the problems of living in two places. The congressman was a young man with a young family, and Isabel lent a sympathetic ear to his problems.

After dinner the men went into another drawing room for cigars and brandy. Many of the ladies went upstairs to tidy up and the rest of them were ushered down a series of corridors to a music room and sun porch where a small band tuned up. Mrs. Messenger made a point of coming over to speak to Isabel.

"At last we are to see this famous portrait of Leo," she said pleasantly.

"Yes," said Isabel.

Mrs. Messenger smiled. "Leo makes so light of it. I think he is just a little embarrassed at having his picture painted."

Isabel smiled too. "He did it only to please his mother. But I think Mrs. Sinclair was right. There are some people who *need* to be painted. A photograph just won't do." She wrinkled her nose a little ruefully. "Of course, that is a point of view one would expect from an artist."

"I agree with you," the other woman said forthrightly. "In fact, I have been thinking of having my husband's portrait done."

"You have?" said Isabel a little lamely.

The men entered the room and Mrs. Messenger rose. "I'll speak to you at some other time, my dear," she said.

"Of course." Isabel's eyes were enormous as she watched Mrs. Messenger cross the room.

The room had filled with people, but there was no sign of Leo. Arthur Stevens came across the floor to talk to Isabel again and people began to dance. It was ten minutes before Leo finally came in, making all the other men in the room look small. He was followed by Ron Messenger. Leo looked around the room, saw Isabel, and began to move in her direction. He was stopped almost immediately by the British ambassador's daughter.

While Isabel talked to Arthur Stevens, Leo talked to Lady Pamela. He looked to be enjoying the conversation very much. Then he took Pamela out onto the dance floor. Isabel resolutely turned her back on them.

Mr. Stevens asked her to dance. The party had become very gay by now and there was a great deal of laughter. Isabel did her best to join in, but it was all pretense until she felt Leo's presence behind her. A second later he put his hand on her arm.

"You've got my girl," he said humorously to Larry Selneck, with whom she was speaking.

"Sorry, Senator," the young congressman returned a little stiffly. Isabel had gathered from their conversation at dinner that he was rather in awe of Leo.

Leo smiled genially and said a few more words. Isabel watched as the congressman began to relax and finally to joke a little. She looked at Leo. It wasn't a deliberate thing, she thought, that potent charm of his. It was simply a matter of native grace radiating effortlessly upon all who came within his orbit.

"Shall we dance?" Leo asked her, and as she turned into his arms, she saw a smiling Larry Selneck go off to find his wife.

The party broke up at eleven-thirty. "I still can't get over how everyone runs home so promptly," Isabel said to Leo in the car. "One minute there is mirth and music, and the next—*poof*—everyone is getting into their coats."

"Getting home to read those reports," he murmured.

Isabel yawned. "Actually, I like the early hours. By eleven-thirty I'm tired."

"Frankly, so am I. Six o'clock comes awfully quickly the next morning." He grinned. "I remember a party once which didn't break up until well after two. It was at the Wisharts' out in Chevy Chase and the guest of honor was Jerry Roget, and Jerry likes a party. Now, the rule for departures is quite rigid: no one leaves before the guest of honor. Jerry was having a grand time and by midnight still showed no signs of wanting to leave. The British and the French ambassadors were asleep on their feet but refused to break protocol and leave before the guest of honor."

Isabel chuckled. "Talk about being a martyr to one's convictions."

"Frank Wishart suggested that they leave, said everyone would perfectly understand. They wouldn't budge."

"Rule Britannia," said Isabel. *"Vive la France."*

"Wishart wound up telling Jerry to get into his car and drive around for a little so the poor souls could escape. Which Jerry did. He returned in good form and the party went on well into the morning."

Isabel threw back her head and laughed. "What a marvelous story. And what a crazy city!"

"Isn't it?"

Silence fell and Isabel wondered if Leo had been at that party with Lady Pamela. She decided she didn't want to know. She wondered what the people tonight thought about her and Leo and decided she didn't want to know that either.

Lady Pamela had asked her a question that had been gnawing away at the back of her brain all evening. What would she do when Leo's portrait was finished and his mother's party was over? She frowned ahead of her into the night and admitted to herself she did not want to go back to New York. But her excuse for staying with Leo would be gone.

"You look almost grim, honey," came his voice, and involuntarily she glanced his way.

"Just tired, I guess."

"Mmm?"

"Actually, I was thinking about what Lady Pamela said."

"Ah." He knew instantly what she meant. They pulled into the drive and he shut the engine off and turned to look at her. "I don't want you to go back to New York," he said flatly.

Isabel's eyes closed very briefly. Until this moment she had not let herself know how afraid she had been that he would simply wish her good luck and kiss her good-bye.

"I don't want to go either," she said softly. "You kissed me for the first time in this car. Remember?"

"I remember." He caught her hand in his and turned it. He warm mouth found her wrist and then followed her arm to the inside of her elbow. Isabel gazed at his bent head and felt suddenly dizzy with a rush of intense emotion. He dropped her hand and opened his car door. Isabel waited until he came around to open her door before she got out. He put an arm around her, and holding her close to his side, he slowly walked her to the door and then up the stairs to bed.

Chapter Eleven

On Saturday morning Isabel finished the portrait. In the afternoon they took a long leisurely drive through the Virginia countryside, stopping at an old inn for dinner. It rained Sunday, so they spent the afternoon in the sitting room with a fire blazing and the papers spread all over.

The warm and quiet sitting room was an island of peace for Isabel. Outside, the rain beat on the pavement and the roof, but in here she was safe. The fire light glowed on Leo's shoulder and arm. Isabel bent her head as she watched him contentedly. Without realizing it, she was storing up memories for the future, the bleak and empty future. But for now, she was happy. A log dropped on the fire and his hair reflected a brighter gold. He read something to her from the paper and she smiled faintly, loving the soft cadences of his voice. He raised his head and his eyes rested for a moment on her face. So blue, she thought, his eyes are so very blue. He held an arm out invitingly, and she went to sit beside him, resting her head in the hollow of his shoulder, her body soft and relaxed against the solid strength of his. Leo murmured in her ear and she smiled a little in reply and then closed her eyes.

Here was peace. Here was security. Here was happiness. The outside world could not intrude. She was safe.

On Wednesday afternoon Leo's mother arrived and Isabel drove to the airport to meet her. Isabel had liked Charlotte Sinclair very much but she wished Leo's mother was not coming to Washington. She wished she was not going to be staying at the house in Georgetown. She wished the portrait was still not finished, and she had weeks and weeks ahead of her to work on it.

None of these feelings appeared on her face, however, as she greeted Leo's mother at the airport.

"Isabel. How lovely of you to come and meet me, my dear." Isabel had forgotten how warm Charlotte Sinclair's smile was, how persuasive her charm could be.

"How was your flight, Mrs. Sinclair?" she asked as they got into Isabel's rented station wagon.

"The flight was fine." Charlotte's face looked briefly strained. "I'm afraid I just don't like to fly," she confessed.

Isabel abruptly remembered how her husband had died. "Of course you don't," she said with brisk sympathy. "It would be a miracle if you did."

"Ben is getting his flying license. I bite my tongue and shiver in abject fear every time he goes up." She sighed. "He's so like his father. He loves planes and he's absolutely fearless."

"Did your husband pilot himself?"

"Yes. He was very good, too. He wasn't at the controls the night they crashed and I've often thought. . . . Oh, well. I don't want to bore you with my problems, dear. Tell me, how are you enjoying Washington?"

"Very much, thank you. The dresses we bought have been perfect."

"I'm so glad. Now tell me, who has Leo invited for Friday night?"

They spent the rest of the drive discussing the upcoming party. Not a word was said about the portrait until they arrived at the house. Then Isabel took Leo's mother into the library, where the portrait still rested on her easel.

Mrs. Sinclair gazed at it a long time in silence. When she finally turned to Isabel, her eyes were suspiciously bright. "Oh, my dear," she said softly. "Oh, my dear."

Isabel looked at her gravely. "You are satisfied?"

"Satisfied—yes. I am satisfied." Mrs. Sinclair turned back to the picture. "I was afraid it was going to be merely pretty," she said. "But it isn't. You've caught it, that special radiance that makes Leo Leo. You've caught it." She turned back to give Isabel a shrewd look. "You've caught something else, too; it shows around the mouth. It's not there on Leo's face very often; he hides it well. But you caught it."

The gravity of Isabel's expression did not alter. "How bad are his knees?"

"I don't think they hurt a great deal now. He's limited, of course, in what he can do. And that is very hard for him to accept. He didn't play for so long on damaged knees because of his great team spirit, you understand. I know Leo too well. He played because he wouldn't admit that he couldn't play."

"So he ended up nearly crippling himself."

"Yes. Stupid, wasn't it? Unforgivable, really, in a man of Leo's intelligence. But there it is. He simply will not admit to pain, not until, quite literally, he can't get to his feet. Which is what happened to him at last."

"What a terrible sport football is!" Isabel was passionately angry. "Why the hell do they do it?"

Mrs. Sinclair sighed. "You're asking the wrong person, my dear. I'm not a male."

"Male," said Isabel scornfully. "It isn't male. It's barbaric!"

"My husband and my sons absolutely adored it. I can't tell you why, but they did. Ben, fortunately, did not have Leo's aptitude." Mrs. Sinclair made a wry face. "So now he's taken up flying instead."

The two women looked at each other for a moment in the silence of perfect accord. Then Isabel looked back to the portrait. "From the way he moves, you'd never be able to tell he had been injured."

"He worked at physical therapy. My, did he work. No, you can't tell. But the cartilage in his knees is irrevocably damaged. The doctors repaired what they could, but it had gone too far." Isabel had seen the scars on Leo's knees but refrained from mentioning this interesting fact to his mother.

"How have people reacted to your painting Leo?" Mrs. Sinclair asked curiously.

"I'm famous," Isabel replied. "Everywhere I go

I'm pointed out as 'the girl whose doing Leo's portrait.' It's going to be my epitaph."

"Nonsense," Mrs. Sinclair said with a smile. "It will merely be your beginning." She looked back to the portrait. "You do very impressive work, Isabel. Very impressive."

"I'm glad you are pleased, Mrs. Sinclair." Isabel smiled. "I like it too," she confessed.

"And so you should. Now I am going upstairs to unpack and perhaps lie down for a little."

"Of course. Leo said to tell you he'd try to get home a little early tonight."

"Good."

Mrs. Sinclair went upstairs and Isabel wandered out to the kitchen and checked the dinner. She then went to the sitting room, where she stared into the empty grate for a very long time.

In fact, Isabel was still sitting on the couch when Leo returned home. He had arrived home early, and the three of them enjoyed a relaxed dinner served by Mrs. Edwards. After dinner they went back into the sitting room. Isabel did not curl up next to Leo on the sofa, but she sat instead in a graceful old wing chair. Mrs. Sinclair was at a small secretary in the corner. She perched her glasses on her nose and took out paper and pen.

"Now, then," she said to Leo, "you engaged the caterer?"

"Yes, Mama."

"The menu?"

"I thought we'd have veal."

"Good idea. Let's see: a clear soup, salad and brie, and dessert?"

"Fine. I'll take care of the wine."

"Good. I'll order the flowers. What florist shall I use?"

"Aster's."

"All right. Now for the difficult part: the seating arrangement."

Leo grinned. "Ah, yes."

Isabel listened with fascination as they went over the entire guest list. Isabel, as guest of honor, would be at Leo's right. She was gratified to notice that Lady Pamela Ashley was put at least halfway down the table. Some of the guests, however, posed distinct problems.

"No, Mama, you can't put Ron next to Mrs. Herries."

"Why not?" Mrs. Sinclair asked.

"She's his daughter's lover's wife."

"Oh. I see." Mrs. Sinclair frowned at her list and came up with another name that was more acceptable.

"I don't believe I heard that properly," Isabel murmured.

Leo chuckled. "I'm sure they'd both behave themselves, but it would be awkward for them. And I wouldn't put Arthur Stevens next to Mrs. Vandergrift. He's been rather brutal lately about fiscal policy at the Federal Reserve."

Mrs. Sinclair's frown tightened. "All right. How is the British ambassador for Mrs. Vandergrift?"

"Fine. Lord Ashley is a grand fellow. You could give him anyone and he'd be right at home."

Mrs. Sinclair smiled. "I'm glad some of your guests are adaptable, Leo."

The seating chart done, they chatted comfortably for another hour. Mrs. Sinclair and Leo did most of the talking. Isabel noticed, with admiration and amusement, that without seeming to press him at all, Mrs. Sinclair found out a great deal about her son's activities.

At ten-thirty Mrs. Sinclair excused herself and went up to bed. As the sound of her footsteps disappeared up the stairs, Leo turned to Isabel with a smile in his eyes. "You can come sit on the sofa now," he said softly.

Isabel didn't move but looked at him, her face serious. "I can't stay here after this weekend," she said. "You must see that, Leo."

"Why not?"

Isabel made a restless movement with her hands. "United States senators do not have live-in girlfriends. If it became known—and, of course, it would—it would damage you very badly back home."

He didn't deny it. "And if I say I don't care?"

"*I* care. I won't do it to you."

"You could marry me instead," he said.

Isabel stared for a minute at his face. It looked set, strained almost. She looked down at her own clasped hands. The knuckles were white with pressure. Panic gripped her stomach muscles. "It wouldn't work," she mumbled. "I'm not the Washington-hostess type."

"You're my type," he said.

She refused to look at him. "No. It wouldn't work."

There was a tense silence. "I see," he said. His voice was quiet. Too quiet. "Well, if you won't be my wife and you won't be my mistress, then I reckon we've come to the end of it."

Isabel's head bent even farther forward so that her long black hair swung in a curtain around her face. "I might get a commission here in Washington." Her voice was almost inaudible.

He rose from the sofa and went to stand in front of the fireplace, his back toward her. "You might," he said flatly. "In fact, my mother is going to some trouble to ensure that you do."

"Mrs. Messenger mentioned something to me the other night." Isabel raised her head and looked at his back. "If I were to paint Mr. Messenger, I'd have to go live with them out in McLean. We could still see each other, couldn't we?"

Leo kept his back to her. There was something very rigid about his body, the legs braced apart a little, head forward.

"You mean you could come by here for visits?"

Isabel felt the hot color come into her face. "Wouldn't you like that?"

"Oh, yes, I'd like that fine." At last he turned and looked at her. His eyes were filled with a cold blue light.

"I can't make a permanent commitment, Leo," she said miserably. She had not known he could look so hard. "I just can't."

An odd expression flitted across his face, softening it, making him look more like the Leo she knew.

"All right, honey." He sounded a little weary. "Have it your way."

She got out of her chair, took two running steps, and then was in his arms. "I love you," she said into his shoulder. "I do. But I'm not the marrying kind, Leo."

He buried one hand in her long hair. "I know," he said. "I understand. The hell of it is, I do understand."

After a long minute she took her face out of his shoulder and looked up. She put her palms on either side of his face. "I don't want to leave you," she said. "You know that, don't you?"

His eyes narrowed and his hands held her shoulders. "Isabel," he said, and bending his head he began to kiss her.

There was an urgency to this kiss that was new, a hunger. Isabel could feel the whole hard length of his body pushing against her. Her mouth opened under his lips. His hands slid down her shoulders to her waist and rested on the curve of her hips. She responded, taking fire from his touch, sliding her hands under his jacket to get closer.

His lips were on her throat, her ear. "Let's go upstairs," he muttered.

"Yes." Neither of them gave a thought to Mrs. Sinclair as they walked, Isabel first, Leo behind, up the stairs to Isabel's bedroom. They were not being circumspect in case Leo's mother came out into the hall. Simply, they couldn't bear to touch each other until they knew they would not have to stop.

The door closed behind them. Isabel turned, standing on tiptoe, and slid her arms around his neck. She felt him pull her sweater out of her skirt and then his hand came up, inside her bra, to caress her breast. She moved a little with the sheer sensual pleasure of it. He raised his head and she gazed up at him.

"Leo." she said, her voice slow and husky. "Leo the lion." She touched his mouth with the tips of her fingers. "How I do love you."

"Show me," he murmured. His eyes were very dark. "Show me how much you love me."

In answer Isabel reached up and began to unbutton his shirt. In less than a minute they were both lying naked on the bed.

He was rougher than he had ever been before as the urgency of his kiss in the sitting room carried over into his lovemaking now. The Isabel of a week ago would have been frightened by such hungriness, but not tonight. Tonight, with the shadow of separation in both their minds, she gave in to the force within him. Blindly, she surrendered her body to him, letting herself remain helpless before him. He overpowered her, overmastered her, and at the starkest limits of surrender she discovered a blazing shuddering fulfillment all her own. Afterward, as she held him in her arms and listened to the wild hammering of his heart, she knew she had possessed him as surely as he had possessed her.

"How can I hold on to you?" His voice in her ear sounded almost fierce.

"We'll work something out," she replied softly. She ran her fingers tenderly through his sweat-streaked golden hair. "I have to move out of the house, but I'm not moving out on you. I won't go back to New York. Something will turn up, I'm sure of it."

He raised himself a little so that he was looking directly into her face. His shoulders looming over her looked enormous and his eyes in the light of the bedside lamp were intensely blue. "I don't give up," he told her. "I have many failings but once I make up my mind, I don't give up. And I've made up my mind about you."

"Leo," she said. "Why?"

He smiled a little crookedly. His breathing had finally begun to slow. "Any other woman who said that would be fishing for a compliment. But not you. You really don't know, do you?"

"No."

He rolled over and lay on his back beside her, looking up at the ceiling. "You're so alive, Isabel. You live your life with more intensity than anyone I have ever known. That's probably why you're such a fine artist."

Isabel turned to look at his profile. "I've been trying not to feel anything these past few years," she protested in bewilderment.

"I know." A very tender smile curled his lips. "You were so frozen you were absolutely fierce with it." His blue eyes smiled at her. "You burned with it, honey. You project more concentrated power in your little finger than most women have in their entire bodies. Why do you think the despicable Philip bothered with you? He was a sophisticated thirty-year-old and you were a schoolgirl."

Isabel had often thought about that. "I don't know," she said hesitatingly. "I imagine he spotted me as easy prey."

"I don't think that was it at all. For what it's worth to you, you probably burned him a lot worse than he did you. Imagine having to settle for an empty society wife after you've had a taste of Isabel."

Isabel laughed. "Leo, you're crazy. But I admit you've made me feel a lot better about 'the despicable Philip.' Just being able to think of him in those terms is a help." She snuggled her head into his shoulder. "I swore a vow of eternal celibacy after Philip," she murmured.

"And you kept it for nine years. That's what I mean. When you do something, honey, you do it all the way."

Isabel smiled. She turned her head so that her lips were against the bare skin of his shoulder. "So do you." She was thinking of his football injuries. "You don't know when to give up."

"No." He sounded serious, almost grim. "I don't."

"Leo, maybe you'd better go back to your room tonight. What will your mother think if she sees you coming out of here in the morning?"

"I'll get up early," he said.

She didn't really want him to go. "All right. If you're sure . . ."

"I'm sure," he said firmly. "Stop worrying and go to sleep."

Isabel closed her eyes. "Yes, Senator," she murmured. And she did.

She awoke before he did the following morning. Leo's back was toward her and she leaned closer and laid her cheek on his shoulder. It was still shocking to wake and find him there, a man in the bed next to her. After a minute he stirred.

"Good morning," he said, and rolled over on his back.

"Good mawnin'."

She watched him try to wake up. He rubbed his tousled hair and yawned. There was golden stubble on his cheeks and chin, and his blue eyes were heavy with sleep.

Isabel put her hands behind her head. "Your mother," she said delicately.

"I know, I know," he grumbled. "I won't besmirch your reputation." He sat up and stretched, shoulder and back muscles flexing with the motion. He got out of bed.

"Damn," he said. "I don't have a change of clothes in here."

"Put a towel around your waist. That way, if you run into your mother, you can pretend you're on your way back from the shower."

He went into the bathroom and in a minute she heard the shower being turned on. When he came out, he was wrapped as she suggested. "Of course," he said, "there *is* a shower in my room, but never mind. I won't meet Mama at this hour." He came over to the bed and bent to kiss her. "Go back to sleep, honey. Now that I'm up, I'm going over to the gym. Mama won't make an appearance until nine, so sleep for a while."

"Will you be back for breakfast?"

"Nope." He grinned. "Important conference this morning." He went to the door, opened it, peered up and down the hall, and then exited, softly closing the door behind him.

Isabel did not go back to sleep but lay, hands behind her head, staring at the door through which he had gone.

She had told Leo she loved him. And she did. How could she not? Leo could not fail of love wherever he touched. She loved him, but she could not marry him.

He had surprised her last night. She had not realized that their relationship was serious for him, that he would go so far as to want to marry her.

It was impossible, of course. There wasn't room in her life for marriage. She couldn't afford the loss of freedom marriage would inevitably entail; she couldn't afford the sheer loss of time and energy. She was an artist and she had always held strong views on the subject of women artists and marriage.

She should have explained all this to Leo, of course. She couldn't imagine why she hadn't. By panicking she had only sounded stupid when in fact she had a very sane, sensible, and logical reason for not wishing to marry him.

He had accepted her stammered rejection without question, however. Perhaps he, too, realized, deep down, the impossibility of a formal union between them. He needed a wife whose interest lay in the same direction as his, a wife who would entertain for him and who would hold his flag high in the eminent world of Washington politics and society. For both their sakes it was better to keep their relationship as it was: strictly voluntary, with room for either of them to back out if, for some reason, the going should get rough.

Chapter Twelve

On Friday night the elite of Washington arrived at Leo Sinclair's home in Georgetown. For the last few days word had circulated that Senator Sinclair's dinner for Isabel MacCarthy was one of The Events of the year's social calendar. The chosen few who were invited consequently looked bright with triumph as they arrived; the cold drizzle seemed to affect nobody's spirits.

Isabel wore a simple ivory sheath dress and looked, as Leo told her, magnificent. Her portrait of him hung in the place of honor in the drawing room above the marble chimneypiece.

Isabel had met nearly everyone present at least once previously, so it was not too difficult to remember who was who. Mrs. Sinclair had filled the drawing room with fresh flowers, and hired maids who assiduously passed canapés and drinks. Most everyone was vociferous in praise of Isabel's portrait.

"You look older, darling," Lady Pamela said to Leo as she gazed at it critically. "There are lines around your mouth."

"Yes. It makes me look quite statesmanlike, I think," Leo replied.

"It's marvelous, Leo," put in Hilda Messenger. "I like it very much."

"Mama is pleased," he returned with perfect good humor. "Now she's got a portrait of her senator son to hang on her walls—like a trophy!"

At nine o'clock Mrs. Sinclair discreetly indicated that dinner was served. Then, led by Leo and Isabel, the guests began to move toward the dining room.

Mrs. Sinclair had outdone herself, Isabel thought. Imposing silver candelabra stood on either end of the long table, and in the center was a lovely arrangement of fresh flowers. Fine silver and china sparkled against white damask in the candlelight.

I could never do this, thought Isabel. She had assisted Leo's mother this afternoon—in fact, she had arranged the centerpiece, but the initiative had all been Mrs. Sinclair's.

Dinner was superb. "I know. They're the best caterers in town," Leo told Isabel imperturbably when she commented on the quality of the food. "Everyone uses them."

As dessert was served, Leo got up to speak. The after-dinner toast, defunct in most of the civilized world, still survived in Washington. Relaxed and informal, he made a toast to Isabel and to art that was both highly complimentary and comfortably humorous.

Isabel felt stiff as she stood up to make the necessary response. She managed a few compliments for Leo as a subject and as a person, and then expressed her gratitude to both Leo and Mrs. Sinclair for assembling such a distinguished group of people to view her effort. She was feeling more comfortable as she finished and sat down amid a general outpouring of smiles.

Shortly after the toast, everyone rose from the table and Mrs. Sinclair led the women back to the drawing room while Leo escorted the men to the library for brandy and cigars. Isabel noticed with interest that Mrs. Messenger was engaged in serious conversation with Mrs. Sinclair. She hoped fervently she would soon receive a commission from the Messengers.

"Did you go to art school in New York, Miss MacCarthy?" said a very cool, very English voice at Isabel's side. Isabel turned to look into the violet eyes of Lady Pamela Ashley.

"Yes," said Isabel. "I did."

"And do you have a studio there now?"

Isabel thought of her crammed bedroom and smiled faintly. "Not really. Not yet, at least. I've got half my paintings stored in a former teacher's studio. I shall really have to get something of my own soon."

"Ah. Then you *are* going back to New York?"

Isabel looked dispassionately at the Englishwoman's lovely face. Two weeks ago she would have frozen up and answered in wary monosyllables. Now she merely raised an eyebrow and said, "Why are my plans of such interest to you, Lady Pamela?"

The British ambassador's daughter shrugged her slender shoulders. She was wearing a simple black gown and her skin looked dazzling against the midnight satin. She made Isabel feel like a gypsy.

"I'm not the only one who is interested," she said in her clipped voice. "There's been some speculation already about you and Leo." The violet eyes were hard on Isabel's face. "You cannot continue to stay here. Leo can't afford it."

Isabel nodded thoughtfully. "I see. You are concerned for the political consequences?"

"Yes," snapped Lady Pamela.

Isabel lifted her chin, grave and graceful in her great natural dignity. "Thank you so much for mentioning your concern to me," she said pleasantly. "I shall bear it in mind." Left with nothing more to say, Lady Pamela glared. Isabel smiled at her a little absently, murmured an excuse, and went over to where Mrs. Sinclair beckoned her. Isabel had come a long way in the last few weeks.

"Isabel dear," Leo's mother said, "Mrs. Messenger has been telling me how much she admires Leo's portrait."

"Yes," Hilda Messenger said. "In fact, I'd like very much for you to do a portrait of my husband, Miss MacCarthy."

"I see," said Isabel quietly, hoping that the triumph she felt was not too clearly visible on her face. "When would you like me to do it, Mrs. Messenger?"

"If you could start right away, that would be perfect. Otherwise we'll have to wait until the fall. We leave for Europe in May."

"I could do it right away. I don't have any plans for the next few months."

"Wonderful," said Mrs. Messenger briskly. "Now as to your fee . . ." and she named a price that was several thousand dollars more than Isabel had gotten for Leo's portrait.

"Fine," Isabel said calmly. She felt like jumping up and down and screaming with joy, but she kept her voice even and businesslike.

"As you don't have your studio in Washington I hope you'll come stay with us out in McLean until you've finished."

"Thank you, Mrs. Messenger. I would like that."

"Monday, then? Shall we expect you on Monday?"

"Monday," repeated Isabel, and smiled. "Certainly."

There was a murmur of male voices outside the drawing-room door and then the men entered the room. Isabel caught Leo's eye almost instantly and raised her eyebrows very slightly. He came across the room to her immediately.

"You look like the cat that's swallowed the canary," he said with amusement. "What happened?"

"I got the commission from Mrs. Messenger." With him she could let down her guard. Her thin face blazed with triumph.

"That's wonderful!" His blue eyes mirrored her expression. "Good for you, honey. You're on your way."

"Yes," she said. "I really think I am. God, I might even be able to get my own studio. At last! A place to work that's all my own. I won't know myself."

A little of the light died out of his eyes. "Where do you work now?" he asked.

"In friends' studios. At school. In my bedroom. Everywhere and nowhere. My paintings are stored in about eight different places." She took a deep breath. "Wow." She grinned at him. "I'm flying."

"And so you should be." He looked across the room at Ron Messenger. "Ron is a fine person. You'll like working with him."

"He'll be a good subject," Isabel said. "He has a good face." She frowned a little thoughtfully as she thought about how she might do him.

There was a little stir by the piano and then Mrs. Sinclair announced that the wife of the Italian ambassador was going to sing. The Fellinis had been Washington fixtures for years and Mrs. Fellini's voice was very well-known. The ambassador played the piano as his wife sang a selection of Italian songs in a clear and well-trained soprano. When she finished, she asked if anyone else would like to sing as well. There were no takers, and after another half an hour of the kind of fluent conversation that Washingtonians never seemed to tire of, it was eleven o'clock and people began to go home. By eleven-thirty the house was empty.

Mrs. Sinclair turned to Isabel as they stood in the drawing room and said, "Well?" Her eyes were twinkling.

Isabel hugged her. "I don't know how I can thank you enough," she said a little breathlessly. "You have been so wonderfully kind to me."

"Nonsense, my dear. I've done Hilda Messenger a great favor."

"Ron is delighted too," said Leo as he came across the room to join them. "He says it's going to be a very patrician experience, having his portrait done. He already feels like Charles the First."

"Oh, dear," said Isabel comically, "I hope he doesn't expect me to paint him on horseback."

Everyone laughed and then Mrs. Sinclair yawned delicately. "Well, good night, children. I need my beauty rest." She kissed them both. "Don't expect to see me before ten tomorrow," she murmured, and giving them a vague and lovely smile, she went off to bed.

"She's a pearl among women, my mama," Leo said affectionately after she had gone.

Isabel looked a little distressed. "Do you think she knows abut us?"

"She doesn't want to know," he said simply.

"Oh."

"As I said, a pearl." He put his hand on her neck, under the heavy weight of her hair. "The portrait was a smashing success. Jim Lewiston was asking me about the rest of your work. I told him to contact you. He's rather a serious collector and he sounded as if he might be in a buying mood."

"Oh, Leo," she breathed reverently.

"That studio appears to becoming closer and closer," he commented. His hand was still on her neck.

There was a long pause. "Well," he said then, "why don't we emulate my revered parent and go to bed?"

She put her hand on his shoulder and reached up to kiss his jaw. "Yes," she said. "Let's."

Mrs. Sinclair left for Charleston on Saturday, taking with her Leo's portrait, carefully crated and wrapped. After returning from church on Sunday, Leo took Isabel golfing once again.

Isabel found it difficult to understand how, under the circumstances, Leo could still go to church. In anyone else she would consider the contradiction hypocritical, but such an explanation didn't occur to her in his case.

"I like to go," he had replied simply when she asked him, and that, she decided, was probably the best explanation she was likely to get.

Isabel discovered that she enjoyed golf very much. With Leo's encouragement she had taken a few lessons during the afternoons, and so she was not as awkward now as she had been previously. She was, of course, nowhere near Leo in proficiency, but one of the pleasures of the game was that you did not have to be the equal of someone to play with them. They played eighteen holes. Leo shot an eighty-four and Isabel a 121, and they both had a splendid time.

"I've never gotten into this physical-fitness craze," Isabel confessed over beers in the clubhouse. "I hate getting all sweaty and untidy. Terribly unfashionable, I know, but there it is. Golfing suits me just fine; its leisurely pace isn't too strenuous and the scenery is great."

"It suits me just fine these days as well," he said. His face was perfectly pleasant, but Isabel detected a note of suppressed bitterness in the soft vowels of his drawl. She felt a sharp stab of pity, which she prudently concealed. The last thing Leo would accept was pity, she understood that perfectly.

"I must say, it has disappointed me in one way, though," she continued talking with scarcely a pause. "Where are all those wonderful names from

P.G. Wodehouse? The mashie, the niblick—you know . . ."

He grinned and the indefinable shadow lifted. "Do you know P. G. Wodehouse's golf stories?"

"I know everything by P. G. Wodehouse. I must confess I like Lord Emsworth and his prize pig best, but I read all the golf stories. His characters are always smashing balls with their mashies. Why don't we have a mashie?"

"Because, being practical Americans, we simply call the woods and irons by numbers. It's much duller, I agree."

"I'm going to call it a mashie," Isabel said firmly. "By the way, which one is a mashie?"

"The number-five iron. And the mashie niblick is the number seven."

"And the niblick?"

"Is the number-eight iron."

Isabel nodded. "I'll bear that in mind. Niblick sounds much nicer."

"It does," he agreed with her cordially.

"I didn't know you were a golfer, Miss Mac-Carthy," said a voice behind Isabel, and she turned to see Ron Messenger smiling down at her.

"How do you do, Mr. Messenger," she replied. "And I certainly wouldn't call myself a golfer. This was my first time all the way 'round, in fact. Leo has been marvelously patient."

"What did you shoot?" he asked her pleasantly.

Isabel made a rueful face. "One-twenty-one."

He raised his eyebrows. "Not bad at all for a first effort."

"That's what I've been trying to tell her," Leo put in.

Ron Messenger smiled at Leo. "Dan Murphy was just telling me that one of the networks is putting together a documentary on your football career."

Leo's face became perfectly expressionless. "Yes. So they've informed me."

"Who's doing the narrative?"

"I have no idea. All the footage they're using was shot a few years ago, and they own it."

Messenger looked surprised. "Aren't they interviewing you as well?"

"They wanted to. I refused."

There was a moment's blank silence, then Isabel said, "What time do you want me to arrive tomorrow, Mr. Messenger?"

He pulled his eyes from Leo's face and looked at Isabel. "Why don't you come around three, Miss MacCarthy. I don't imagine you will want to start until the following day."

"Three will be fine," Isabel said, and smiled.

"Well, I have a group waiting for me," Ron Messenger said easily. "We'll see you tomorrow then, Miss MacCarthy."

Leo rose to his feet, hand held out. "Good seeing you, Ron. Enjoy your game."

Messenger's face relaxed imperceptibly as he shook Leo's hand. After he had left, Leo slowly sat back down.

Isabel sipped her beer and didn't say anything for a long time. Leo was quiet also, staring with seeming intensity at his hands. Isabel looked at his hands as well. They were big, square-fingered hands, hard and competent. But for all their size and strength, the fingers were finely drawn. They were the sort of hands, Isabel thought, that a sculptor would love.

"Do you hate it so much?" she asked softly, breaking the silence.

He stared still at his hands. "Yes," he said briefly, "I do."

"Why?"

"Because," said Leo, lifting his eyes, "they're going to make a damn melodrama out of it. All this crap about my gallantry and playing in pain. Christ!" His eyes were savage.

"I couldn't agree more," Isabel said astringently. "It wasn't heroism; it was stupidity. Hardly the sort of behavior one should hold up to young boys to emulate."

The blue eyes were now directly on hers. "Oh?" he said.

"It was an act of colossal egotism, I should say. One can only hope you have advanced in maturity since then."

"One can only hope," he repeated. Laughter lines creased the corners of his eyes.

"Since you can't stop the documentary, however," Isabel went on relentlessly, "your wisest course is to rise above the whole thing by simply ignoring it."

By now he was laughing. "I had the same thought," he gasped.

"Good." She smiled at him sweetly. "Golf is much more civilized."

He had regained his composure. "It is, honey," he said, blue eyes brilliant. "It most certainly is."

It was the last night of Isabel's stay in the old

Georgetown house she and Leo made the most of
every minute. Deep in the night, when Leo had
finally fallen asleep, Isabel lay awake and thought
back to the incident in the clubhouse that
afternoon.

It was a thousand pities that there had to be a
documentary. Isabel didn't doubt that Leo would
be treated as a hero. It would be a prospect most
men would adore—the chance to be sancitified and
lionized before a national TV audience. Most poli-
ticians would sell their eyeteeth for the chance.

Leo would hate the show because it would reveal
his physical infirmity to millions. Yet there was
more to it than that, Isabel realized. For all his
charm and his instinct for human relations, Leo
was a deeply private man. He did not object to
sharing his public persona with his fans or with his
constituents, but his personal problems and ago-
nies he wanted kept private. Isabel could understand that perfectly. She looked over at the silky
fair hair lying tousled on the pillow at her side.
Tomorrow night he wouldn't be there. Resolutely
she beat down the wave of desolation that swept
through her at that thought, closed her eyes, and
tried to go to sleep.

Chapter Thirteen

Isabel settled in at the Messengers' McLean estate the following day and on Tuesday began to paint Ron Messenger. Her sessions with him were extremely interesting. He was polished and urbane and smacked of old family, New England prep-school, and Harvard, yet there was something very real about him that Isabel liked very much. His interests were art, architecture, and antiques, and his conversation was both enjoyable and stimulating.

Hilda Messenger was a little too much the professional Washington wife for Isabel to feel completely at ease with her. She was a highly polished specimen of a highly polished type, and she made Isabel feel her her own rough edges too acutely. But Isabel had to admit that she was very pleasant and went out of her way to be kind.

It would have been an ideal situation, in fact, were it not for Leo. Or rather, the lack of Leo.

Finding time with Leo alone did not prove as easy a task as Isabel had anticipated. The Messengers were very social people and they expected to include Isabel in most of their activities. It was absolutely awful, seeing Leo in the busy whirl of a dinner party, and then leaving him to go home with the Messengers.

It wasn't until Sunday that they had the chance to be together. Isabel told the Messengers that she and Leo were going to golf and then have dinner. Leo picked her up at one o'clock and they went, not to Chevy Chase, but back to Georgetown. They spent the afternoon in bed.

"This is an impossible setup," Leo said later. Much later, the sun had set and it was dark outside.

"I know," said Isabel dismally. "I didn't reckon on the ferocious Washington social instinct when I made my brilliant plan." She turned her head to look at him. "I felt like a sixteen-year-old sneaking out to meet a forbidden boyfriend today," she said with an attempt at humor.

His lips smiled, but his eyes darkened. He picked up her hand and began to play idly with her fingers. "How is the portrait coming?"

"Very well. Ron is a darling. I'm having fun doing him."

"That's good."

"Oh, Leo," she said miserably and, turning, buried her face in his shoulder. "It's all such a mess. I can't stay here like this. It's impossible."

"Yes." He sounded tense. "It is."

"I'll be finished with Ron in another week. The work is going well."

"I see."

She sat up and shoved her hands into her hair, pushing it back off her face. "I'll have to go back to New York," she said flatly. "At least for a while."

He didn't say anything.

"I *have* to, Leo," she said a little desperately. "My

work is back there. Even if I got another commission, I can't keep on doing portraits indefinitely. That's only a small part of what I want to do. You can understand that, can't you?"

"Oh, yes, I understand." He put his hands behind his head and regarded her with veiled blue eyes. "I own half an island," he said, seemingly at random. "It's off the coast of Island Views. Ben and the development company own the other half, but I wanted to keep a part for myself. I spent the whole summer there last year. It's not modern at all; in fact, it's pretty primitive. But it's totally private and quiet. Ben hasn't even started developing the other half yet."

It was very quiet in the room. "Yes?" said Isabel.

"Would you come and spend the summer with me?" he asked.

"Oh, Leo." She smiled, radiant. "Oh, darling, I'd love that."

The shadowy look about his mouth lifted. "Would you, honey? It's not much more than a shack."

She laughed. "Then I'll be right at home. The plumbing can't be worse than it was in the apartment I grew up in." She put her hands on his shoulders and bent over him.

"Plumbing?" he said. "Who said anything about plumbing?"

"Leo!" Isabel's eyes widened in horror.

"I said it was primitive."

"Oh, well," Isabel said resignedly, and bent down to kiss him lightly. Her black hair fell about them like a tent. "You Tarzan, me Jane."

He chuckled. "There's plumbing. And electricity too."

She pulled back a little. "Then why tease me?"

He slid his hands into the heavy silk of her hanging hair. "I just wanted to see how much you loved me," he murmured.

"Very much," she said softly, and bent forward to kiss him. "Very much indeed . . ."

The conversation ended for quite some time.

It was April when Isabel finally got back to New York. The apartment, when she let herself in, looked like a place remembered from another life: strange and familiar all at once. She was in the middle of unpacking when Bob came home.

"Isabel!" He gave her an affectionate hug when she came out into the hall to greet him. "How are you, stranger?" he asked.

"Fine." Their eyes were almost on a level and she smiled into his. "How are *you*?" She frowned. "You look like you put on weight."

"Thanks a lot," he retorted. "I'm not even in the door and she's telling me I'm fat."

"I didn't say that. The extra weight is very becoming."

"Liar." He gave her a look of mock injury. "It's all the meals I've been eating out."

"Italian food," Isabel said instantly. She knew his weakness.

"I've been at Mama Theresa's four nights a week," he confessed with a grin.

"There's nothing in the refrigerator. I already checked. What did you plan to do for dinner tonight? Mama Theresa?"

"No. Tonight we are going to Gramont's for dinner." This was said very firmly and Isabel's eyes flew open.

"Bob! That's a fortune!"

"I know," he said complacently. "But as you are now a famous painter and I am a junior partner, I think we can afford it."

Isabel's face lit with pleasure. "Bob, you got the promotion. That's great. By all means, Gramont's it is."

They ran into one of the senior partners from Bob's firm at the restaurant, and he insisted that Isabel and Bob join him and his wife for dinner. The senior partner had a difficult time taking his eyes off Isabel, commenting at least four times on how well she was looking. The senior partner's wife spent her time extolling the virtues of marriage. Isabel and Bob bore up as best they could, but the dinner was not the one they had envisioned.

"Well, at least we didn't have to pay," Isabel remarked to Bob in the taxi on the way back home. The senior partner had insisted on picking up the check.

"True." His voice sounded a little muffled and she turned to scrutinize his profile. "Don't mind Mrs. Shore," she said softly.

He made a visible effort to shake off his preoccupation. "I thought Mr. Shore was going to eat you up," he said humorously.

Isabel laughed.

"There is something different about you, Isabel," Bob went on. "I noticed it right away. It's as though all those banked fires have suddenly burst into flame."

"Oh, dear," said Isabel, and bit her lip.

He didn't say anything until he had paid off the taxi and they were walking together into their apartment building. "Is it a man?" he asked then, quietly. She darted a quick look at his face. "You don't have to tell me if you'd rather not," he said evenly.

"Yes," she said. "It is a man." There was a pause. "As a matter of fact, it's Leo Sinclair."

"Leo Sinclair!" He stopped abruptly and stared at her. Then he began to laugh.

"What's so funny?" she asked mildly.

"You are," he said. "How serious is this?"

He opened the apartment door and they both walked into the entrance hall. "I'm going to spend the summer with him on an island in South Carolina."

"On an island in South Carolina. God," he said, "I'll be a blimp by the time you get back."

Isabel didn't know whether she should feel glad or sorry at his instant assumption that she would indeed be coming back.

Isabel rented a loft on New York's Lower East Side and spent the spring months organizing her paintings. It was absolute bliss working in her own place. For the first time in her life, she told Bob, she felt like a professional.

She missed Leo and kept herself busy in order to hide the ache. In the back of her mind always was the promise of the summer.

At the beginning of July Isabel left for Hampton Island. She flew into Savannah and Leo met her at the airport. They left the car at one of the Island

Views docks and boarded a small boat moored nearby. Isabel's luggage filled one-half of the tiny vessel.

"There's no regular ferry service to the island," Leo told her as he started the boat's motor. "Not yet, at least. Once Ben gets moving, of course, there will be."

"No cars?" asked Isabel.

He smiled. "No cars."

"Sounds blissful," she said, and leaning back in the boat, she let her eyes devour him.

He had already been on the island a week, he had told her, trying to get things shipshape. He was very tanned and his hair looked even lighter than she remembered. When she first saw him at the air-port, her heart had given a tremendous leap and it hadn't quite calmed down yet. They had greeted each other casually, conscious of possible watching eyes, and their conversation thus far had been such that it could have been overheard without embarrassment by a roomful of total strangers.

The trip to the island took ten minutes. Isabel gazed at the surrounding water, marsh, and sky when Leo's voice said, "There's the island. Over yonder."

Oveh yondeh. How she had missed the sound of his voice. She looked obediently to where he was pointing, and in another minute they reached a small dock. The air was filled with the scent of pine.

Leo tied the boat up and, balancing easily, stepped up onto the dock.

"Can you hand me up your luggage?" he asked.

"Sure," said Isabel, and reached up her cases; most of them contained painting equipment. Then he held out his hand to her. When she landed on the dock next to him, he reached out with his other hand and pulled her close.

"I missed you," he said fiercely, and kissed her, hard and long.

"I missed you too," she said breathlessly when finally he released her. "June went by so slowly."

"That it did." He moved from her with obvious reluctance. "Well, let me show you our palatial estate."

"My bags?" said Isabel, and gestured.

"No trouble, ma'am," he drawled. "We just pile them in this little old wheelbarrow here," which he proceeded to do efficiently, "and we're on our way."

Isabel laughed as she followed him up the sand-and-shell road into the pines. He pushed the wheelbarrow before him with a jaunty cockiness that she loved.

"This is how we get the groceries from the boat to the house," he informed her.

"My God," said Isabel. "Do you have to go to the mainland for all your food?"

"Yep. There's a developer's office on the other side of the island and there are cabins here and there, but they're all deserted. It's been years since the last families moved away from here."

"What happened?" she asked.

"No jobs. There used to be farms here—and fishing, of course. But the young didn't want to stay and the pines grew back over the farmland."

Isabel saw a small cabinlike house appearing in front of them. It looked a lot more substantial than she had been led to believe. There was a screened porch on the front, and inside, Isabel discovered three rooms: a living room, bedroom, and kitchen. The furniture was old and solid. There was a stall shower in the bathroom. The walls in the living room were paneled in white pine.

"This is lovely," Isabel said as she walked around. "Did you build it?"

"No. It's been here for years. I've done some renovations, that's all."

"I love it," she said.

He stood against the door watching her. "I kind of thought you might," he said, drawling a very little more than usual.

Isabel gazed at him, her dark eyes luminous in her thin, intense face. "I love you," she said.

His shoulders came away from the door in a kind of a lunge and then he was across the room and holding her in his arms. Isabel closed her eyes and stopped thinking. Her whole life seemed to have narrowed down to this room, this man, this moment. His mouth was hard on hers, his hands moving possessively over her breasts, her waist, her hips. She felt his desire, felt also the unnamable, irresistible force in him that called so strongly to something in her. Her head was pressed back against his shoulder and his lips left her mouth and moved, searingly, to her exposed throat.

"Isabel," he muttered. "God. Isabel." And suddenly she was swept by fire. Her whole body shuddered and she clung to him fiercely. They almost didn't make it into the bedroom.

"Would you like to go down to look at the beach?" he asked softly a very long time later.

She had been sleepily watching him in the golden

sunlight of late afternoon, and now she raised heavy eyelids and smiled faintly. "If you like."

He stretched and stood up. "Yes," he said. "I want to show you. You'll love it."

God, Isabel thought, watching him. I wish I were a sculptor. "All right," she said, and with some reluctance got out of bed herself.

They walked down another path through the pines and came out on a wide and silver beach. The surf rolled in blue splendor and the dead stumps of trees scattered here and there rose in fantastic formation across the wide sweep of sand. It would make a wonderful painting.

Isabel was very quiet. "It's marvelous," she said at last.

He looked pleased and, without speaking, held out his hand. Isabel put hers in it and together they walked along the water's edge, talking in the low unhurried voices of perfect intimacy. They walked for almost an hour before they returned to the house for a late dinner, after which they retired immediately to bed.

They swam together for the first time the following morning. Isabel had bought a flowered maillot suit in Altman's before she left New York; its deep and dramatic hues suited both her figure and her coloring. Leo wore light blue bathing trunks and she looked appraisingly at his shoulders and arms as they walked down to the beach.

"I should have thought you'd burn, you're so fair," she commented.

"I watch it the first few times I'm out, and then

I'm okay," he said. He was a beautiful golden color and Isabel smiled ruefully.

"I have never even had a red nose," she said. "I start off the summer tanner than most people are by the end of it."

"Don't brag," he said, and Isabel raised her arm and regarded the smooth olive-toned flesh. She sighed.

"I'm not. I've always wanted to be pale and pretty."

"You are neither."

"So gallant, Senator," she murmured.

"You're not at all pretty," he continued peacefully. "You're beautiful. It's a very different thing."

Isabel grinned. "It's also in the eye of the beholder, but I thank you, sir. You have redeemed yourself."

Reaching the beach, they dropped their towels on the sand and went down to the water's edge. There was a mild surf and the water was warm.

Isabel was not a strong swimmer, and she spent most of her time diving through the waves and riding the bigger ones up onto the beach. After playing with her for a while, Leo went out beyond the surf and began to swim. He struck off parallel to the shoreline, and after a few minutes Isabel went back to sit on the beach and watch him. He came out of the water half an hour after she did.

Handing him a towel, Isabel watched as he toweled his hair dry. His golden-brown flesh was glistening with drops of water, and his breathing was only a little faster than normal. He had swum a very long way down the beach and then back.

"Did that feel good?" she asked, and he grinned and dropped down beside her.

"Yep. How about you?"

"I love the water. I don't swim very well—I can do about the length of a pool before I poop out—but I love the surf. When I was a little girl, my folks used to take me to Rockaway on the weekends. We'd make a picnic lunch and take the subway. My father and I would be in the water all day." Her face was bright with remembrance. "My mother used to call us water rats."

She drew her knees up and rested her chin on them. "One summer, when I was ten, we took a bungalow at Breezy Point for two weeks. The beach there is fantastic. Daddy used to say, You can travel the world over, but you'll never find anything better than the Long Island beaches." Her face changed, and so did her voice. "Then Mother got sick."

"How long was she sick?"

"Eighteen months. They gave her the works—chemotherapy, radiation. All it did was make her terribly sick. And then she died anyway. Daddy never got over it. Never."

"That was his failure, not yours."

"I suppose." She drew in a deep, uneven breath. "I haven't thought of that vacation at Breezy Point for years."

"It isn't good to remember only the unhappy things," he said.

She turned her head so that her cheek rested on her knees and her eyes were looking at him. "No, it isn't. In fact, it should be the other way around, shouldn't it?"

"I reckon it should be, honey." There was a note of tenderness in his voice. "I reckon it should be."

The month of July passed, perfect in sunshine, drenched in love. Isabel painted every morning on the beach, and she knew she was doing the best work of her life. Leo had a veritable library of books and reports he wanted to get through, so he would stretch out next to her in a sand chair, read, and make notes while she painted. After lunch they would swim. Sometimes Leo did chores around the house and sometimes they took the boat out and fished or went over to Island Views to shop or play golf. It was an idyll out of time, and it wasn't until they were a week into August that Isabel began to think of the future as well as the present.

Time. It was the snake in the garden, she thought as she sat in a mainland laundromat one hazy August afternoon, watching the clothes going around in the dryer. If only the summer could be like that dryer, she thought, endlessly going around, never forward.

There was a click and the dryer went off. Isabel sighed. "Nothing's eternal, I guess," she said out loud, and went to remove and fold the clothes. She was just finishing when Leo came in. He had been to the supermarket while she did the laundry.

He carried the basket of clothes out to the car for her and they drove back to where Leo had docked the boat. It was after five by the time they got back to the island and had everything put away in the cabin.

Leo went out onto the porch to look at the sky.

"It's going to storm," he said to Isabel. "How about a walk before dinner?"

"Okay," she replied, and they both left the house and strolled along in companionable silence down to the beach, looking at the gathering clouds in the sky.

"Do you still have the car keys?" he asked her suddenly. She had been the one to lock up the car before getting into the boat.

She put her hand into the pocket of her seersucker shorts. "Yes. I do."

He put out a hand. "Better give them to me now, while we're thinking of it. I don't want to spend another hour searching for them because we've both forgotten where they were."

Isabel stared at that strong, brown hand. A few lines from Andrew Marvell went through her head like a refrain:

> But at my back I always hear
> Times wingèd chariot hurrying near.

Quite suddenly she felt the need for action.

"Try and get them," she said, and laughing, took off down the beach. She glanced around quickly to see if he was following her and then she raced along the hard-packed sand. It was a full minute before she realized she was running alone. She slowed down a little, stopped, and then turned to look for Leo.

He stood a hundred yeards up the beach from her, hands in the pockets of his summer slacks, staring out at the water. Watching him, Isabel felt her throat constrict painfully.

He couldn't catch her. He was one of the fastest-running backs ever to play the game of football, and he couldn't catch her. Damn, thought Isabel violently. Damn, damn, damn. Why did I have to run?

Very slowly she walked up the beach until she was near enough to see his profile. He looked very calm. His hands, she noticed, were still in his pockets.

"You'll get no sympathy from me," she said fiercely. "None. You did it to yourself."

"I know." He sounded weary. "But strangely enough, that doesn't make it any better."

Abruptly Isabel turned her back on him. After a minute she began to walk very slowly back the way she had come.

"Isabel." His hand was on her shoulder, forcing her to turn to face him, revealing to him what she had hoped to conceal: the drenching tears that were pouring uncontrollably down her cheeks.

"Oh, honey," he said softly. "Don't." And he took her in his arms.

She turned in to him and reached her arms around his waist to hold him tight. "Does it still hurt?" she wept into his shoulder.

"The psychological pain is much worse than the physical," he said into her hair. "And as you so justly pointed out, the fault is mine alone."

In answer she pressed closer to him and shivered. A few fat raindrops fell on their heads. There was the sound of thunder in the air.

"The storm is starting," Leo said. "Come on, we'd better get back to the cabin."

It was raining hard by the time they reached the house, a heavy tropical rain that soaked them through. They went into the bedroom, and as the storm raged and the thunder crashed, they made love with a passion that was scarcely less wild and primitive than the elements outside.

At last the thunder and lightning subsided, leaving only the rain. Leo flung open the bedroom windows and the sound and smell of the rain filled the room. Isabel lay back against the pillow and watched him.

But at my back I always hear— No! she thought. I wont' think about that. I'm only going to think about now.

Leo came back to the bed and she smiled and held her arms out to him. Lying down beside her, he buried his face in the smooth hollow between her breasts. Isabel ran her hand through the golden tangle of his hair, listening to the rain.

Nothing can take this away from me, she thought. No matter what happens, I'll always have the memory of this moment.

Chapter Fourteen

❧

Isabel had worked on two oils during the summer and they were almost finished. She also had innumerable sketches for future work in her studio.

"Summer is almost over," Leo said to her one day when he returned from a trip to the post office on the mainland. "Tuition bills for September are due."

Isabel was cleaning her brushes in the kitchen. Leo watched her from the doorway.

She cleared her throat. "Whose tuition do you pay? Paige's?"

"No. My mother takes care of Paige's. There are a few other kids I help out. But I don't want to talk about tuition."

Isabel stared down at her brushes. *But at my back I always hear* . . . The famous words rang in her ears and she knew she would have to come to terms with them. "No," she said, "I suppose not." She rinsed the brush, put it down to dry, and turned to face Leo.

"It's time we talked about the future." His voice, like his face, was quiet and grave.

Isabel could feel a hard knot begin to tighten inside her stomach. She swallowed. "The future?"

"The future." He remained in the doorway so the width of the kitchen separated them.

"What do you want to say?"

"For God's sake, Isabel!" Her hand briefly touched her forehead and his voice steadied. She could hear the effort he was making to keep calm. "I love you," he said. "I want you to marry me."

"Oh, Leo," she said. In the afternoon light her face looked pinched and sallow. "I thought we had this out before."

"I was hoping," he said steadily, "that you had changed your mind."

"I'm not the sort of wife you need. I wasn't reared on embassy garden parties and dinner at the White House. I'd only be a liability to you. If you can't see that, I can."

"No, I can't see that at all. You sailed through Washington like a queen." His voice changed. "But I don't give a damn about all that, and you know it. I don't want a hostess and a dinner date. I want a wife. I want you."

Isabel walked past him, out of the kitchen and into the living room, where she stood in front of a large window that looked out toward the water. She remained there, her slim back to Leo. The curve of her slender brown neck as she bent her head, the density of the shining black braid she had wound around her head like a coronet for coolness, entranced him. He could fit his hands around her entire waist, he thought as he watched her. He could *make* her do as he wanted. For a brief frightening minute Leo had an intimation of brutality totally alien to his nature.

"I can't," said Isabel. She turned to face him. "I just can't."

"You said you loved me."

"I do!" There was a glitter in her eyes, and for a moment Leo saw a wild and hunted thing finally brought to bay. "I do love you. I'll never love anyone else. But I can't marry you, Leo."

"I must be extraordinarily stupid"—the bitterness in his voice was clear—"but I don't understand."

She clasped her hands together in front of her. "Leo," she said. "I'm an artist. I want to paint. Can't you understand that?"

"Yes, I think I'm capable of understanding that. What I cannot understand is why you can't paint and marry me as well." Her eyes were dark with distress and his voice deepened, becoming ineffably tender. "Isabel. Honey, I would never stand in the way of your painting. I'll build you the finest studio any artist ever had. We can move out into the country, to McLean or to Chevy Chase . . ."

She was slowly shaking her head and he stopped speaking. The room was very quiet. "Do you know why there were so few great women artists in the past?" Isabel asked, her eyes on her clasped hands.

"Why?"

She raised her eyes to look at him. "Because women married," she said quietly. "They married and became someone's wife and someone else's mother, and all that concentrated energy one needs to expend on art dissipated into something else." He didn't answer. "I saw an interview with Katharine Hepburn a while back," she went on. "She put it very well, I think. You have to make a choice, she said. If you want to succeed as an artist, you must have the courage to stand alone. You can't have your cake and eat it too."

"Very profound." His eyes were intensely blue and there was a white line around his mouth.

"I've put it badly," said Isabel. "But what she said is true. One must make a choice. And I know you, Leo. You'd want a family; you *should* have a family. If ever a man was born to be a father, it's you. But I wasn't born to be a mother. Or a wife. I was born to be an artist."

"I see." His voice sounded unusually clipped. "Well, if that is the case, there's nothing more to say, is there?"

Isabel took a step toward him. "We don't have to say good-bye forever. I didn't mean that."

"You mean you are willing to continue to sleep with me, you just don't want to be my wife." Isabel halted. "Well, that isn't good enough for me, Isabel. I'm sorry, but it just isn't good enough."

She could feel herself growing pale. "Oh," she said. Helplessly, pleadingly, she began, "Leo . . ."

He left the house, closing the door behind him with a gentleness born of violence precariously controlled.

It was dark when Leo returned. He was calm and polite and pleasant, and it was as though a wall of ice had been erected between them. Isabel served dinner and made conversation. He ate and answered her with unfailing courtesy. He dried the dishes as he had done on every other night of the summer, and then sat down at the desk in the living room to write out checks. When he was addressing envelopes, Isabel spoke.

"Leo? Please don't be like this." She crossed the room to stand in front of him. The lamp on the desk illuminated his hair and face. There were threads of gold spangled across his forehead.

"How do you want me to be?" he asked patiently.

"Can't we at least keep what we had?" she asked, and looked down into his eyes. It was like speaking to a man she hardly knew but with whom she was terribly in love.

He shrugged. "What did we have, Isabel? It was a nice summer, but now it's over."

He would not be placated. There was nothing she could do. Isabel went to bed and pretended to be asleep when Leo finally came in. She lay awake for a long, long time, listening to his quiet breathing, feeling the loneliness of being shut out from him. She wanted to reach out to him. She wanted to be held by him and loved and comforted. But she couldn't even touch him. It was like sleeping with a stranger.

The following morning she told him she was returning to New York. He helped her pack and drove her to the airport. ·

New York. Bob. Her own studio. Her own life.

September went by, and October. It was all loneliness, bitter, bitter loneliness.

In November one of the TV stations aired the documentary on Leo. Isabel and Bob watched it together.

There was Leo as a college junior, so very young looking. There was a shot of his parents in the stands watching a football game, and Isabel saw Mrs. Sinclair next to a big, broad-shouldered, good-looking man. So that was Leo's father. That was where he got his size, she thought.

There was a picture of Leo receiving the Heissman Trophy. He looks so young, so golden, she thought. Leo the lion.

Then there were the pro games. "God," said Bob, "but he was the best. Look at that, Isabel. Look at him go through that field."

"Yes," Isabel said. "I see."

Of course they talked about his knee injuries just as Leo had foreseen. If he was watching, though Isabel doubted that he was, he would be hating every minute.

Bob turned the set off, sat down, and looked at her.

"I still can't understand why he did it," she said. The last football shot of Leo in obvious agony as he unsuccessfully tried to get to his feet had shaken her badly.

"You saw how he played, Isabel," Bob said gently. "Perhaps once in a generation you get a Leo Sinclair." He paused. "If you developed arthritis in your hands," he said, "would you continue to paint until you quite literally could no longer move your fingers?"

Isabel's eyes were very bright. "Yes," she said, and finally understood.

November passed. Isabel worked every day at her studio. She had sold several paintings; her name was beginning to be talked of seriously in art circles. A few dealers were recommending her to their clients as a "good investment."

She had an offer for one of the Hampton Island

paintings. She refused to sell it and the offer went higher. It was like a dream; last year at this time she would have been thrilled to receive a tenth of what was now being offered.

Her work since the summer had not gone well. Technically, it was brilliant, but the glow, the magic, the vision that had made the Hampton Island paintings so extraordinary were gone. Nothing could destroy the drawing skill or the exquisite brushwork, but even if she might fool others, Isabel could not fool herself. Something was lost.

And all the time, no matter where she was or what she was doing, there was an acute and overwhelming sense of loss. Painting didn't help. Painting the way she was painting now made it worse.

I did this to myself, she would think. This was my decision. And Leo's words when she accused him of the same thing would come back to her: "I know. But strangely enough, that doesn't seem to make it any better."

The Christmas season was upon them. Isabel and Bob bought a tree and Isabel decorated the apartment with vases of holly. Bob's firm had its Christmas party, which they attended together but after the intellectual sharpness of Washington, Isabel found the New York festivities silly and boring.

The day after the party was Sunday, a day Bob usually slept late. Isabel got up at eight o'clock, went out to the kitchen, and found him at the breakfast table drinking coffee. He was wearing a sweatsuit.

"Are you going running?" she asked in surprise.

"I've been. I just got back."

"My, you're energetic." She belted her robe more

firmly around her waist and went to the stove to pour herself a cup of coffee.

"I couldn't sleep," he said.

"Oh?" She sat down across from him. Isabel had not slept well either, but then that was nothing new.

"Isabel," Bob said, "we've got to talk. About us."

She looked at him gravely. "All right."

"It's something I've been thinking for a while, ever since you came home in September looking like grim death." Isabel stared at her coffeecup. "You said then you wouldn't marry Sinclair because marriage would interfere with your work," Bob went on. "And I've said I needed to live with you because of my work. And we're both liars, Isabel. We're both hiding." His voice was very calm and very clear. Each phrase was spoken deliberately. "We're both afraid."

Isabel pushed her coffeecup away and, putting her elbows on the table, rested her forehead on her hands. Her face masked from his view, she said, "What do you mean?"

"I know something about you, Isabel. We've been friends for many years. And I know how your father's alcoholism has affected you. You're afraid, honey. You're so afraid to trust a man. You're afraid to trust Sinclair, that's why you won't marry him."

Honey. Bob never called her honey. Isabel's breath came painfully.

"And what are you afraid of, Bob?" she asked.

"The truth about myself. I've hidden the truth from the firm, I've hidden it from my family, and most of all, I've tried to hide it from myself." He met her eyes directly. "All these years I've said to myself, maybe I'll change, maybe one day Isabel and I *will* get married. I've hidden behind you, Isabel. For all these years, I've hidden behind you."

"I see," she said. Her voice was very gentle.

"And then, last night, when Mrs. Barrows talked about our getting married, I knew." The room was very quiet. "I knew then that there was no way I was every going to marry you or anyone else."

There was a painful line between his brows. "Is there someone special?" she asked softly.

"Yes."

Isabel put out her hand. "I love you," she said. "My parents never gave me a brother, but I found one in you."

The line between his brows smoothed out. He reached out and covered her hand with his. "I love you too," he said.

Isabel sniffed and he released her. "I need a tissue," she said, and went to the sink to get one.

"Your work has been lousy ever since you got back home," he said to her back.

Isabel blew her nose. "I know."

"Those things you did this summer were the best you've ever done."

Isabel's voice was muffled. "I know," she said again.

"You have to *feel* to be an artist, Isabel. You have to be open to life."

Isabel turned to look at him. "What should I do?" she asked helplessly.

"Marry Sinclair."

"What if he doesn't want me anymore?"

"You'll never know, will you, unless you ask."

Isabel pushed her hair behind her ears. "I'm going to get dressed," she said. "I need to walk."

"Go ahead. And think about what I've just said."

She did think about it. She walked with hands in pockets and bent head, totally unaware of her surroundings, and she thought. And, without conscious direction, her steps took her to the doors of St. Mark's Catholic Church. Before she had a chance to change her mind, Isabel went in.

Mass was in progress and Isabel slipped into a rear pew. The congregation was coming back from Communion and she rose with them for the final prayers. When the church had emptied, she moved forward to the altar.

There was a crèche scene on the altar steps with Mary and Joseph kneeling on either side of the empty manger, watched over by angels and shepherds. She knew the baby would be put in the manger on Christmas Day.

"Look, Isabel!" she could hear her mother's voice saying. "Look! The Baby Jesus is born."

Isabel knelt in the front pew and bowed her head. The familiar smell of the church surrounded her. Why do all Catholic churches smell the same? she thought. She hadn't been inside one in years and yet she would know the smell anywhere.

You're afraid to trust Leo, Bob had said. That had perhaps been true in the spring; it wasn't true anymore. She was no longer afraid that Leo would betray her as her father had. She wasn't afraid of any failing in Leo at all.

The church somehow brought her parents very close to her. She remembered how her father would give her a quarter for the collection basket on Sunday. She remembered her mother's face the day she made her First Communion.

She looked at the statue of Mary on the altar and thought about her mother. She thought of what her mother had suffered and about what her mother's death had done to her father.

It was true that she was afraid, not of Leo, but of loving Leo. All her fine philosophy had been a cover-up for one simple fact: she was petrified of being hurt as her father had been. Loving someone left you so terribly vulnerable. What if Leo should die . . .

You coward, she said to herself. You poor, stupid, ignorant coward. She looked at the scene on the altar. Mary didn't say no, she thought. When the angel appeared to her, she didn't hesitate. "My soul doth magnify the Lord," she had said to Elizabeth. My soul will never magnify anything, Isabel thought. It's been too busy huddling in a corner.

The church began to fill up for the next Mass, so Isabel got up and left. She didn't need public prayer right now. She needed to go home and write a letter to Leo.

Isabel couldn't put pen to paper fast enough when she got home, and the letter was posted Monday morning. "If it's all over, don't bother to reply," she had written. "I'll understand."

The Christmas mails were slow, and she had sent the letter to Charleston. He should get it by Thursday, she reckoned. She couldn't expect a phone call before Thursday . . . if a phone call came.

On Wednesday night she and Bob were sitting in front of the TV watching a Christmas special when the doorbell rang. "I'll get it," Bob said, and left the room. Isabel kept her eyes on the screen even though her thoughts were hundreds of miles away.

She heard the door open.

"You must be Bob," a familiar and well-loved voice said. "I'm Leo Sinclair."

Isabel quite literally stopped breathing.

"Come in, Senator. She's in the living room." Bob's voice came to her through the wild tapping of her heart.

Then Leo stood in the doorway, big and vibrant and lightly sprinkled with raindrops. Isabel was on her feet.

"Leo?" she said. She took one step across the room. He didn't say anything, he just looked at her. Then she began to run.

His arms around her felt so strong. She had thought she would never feel them again. She locked her own arms around his neck and looked up into his face.

"It's you," she said. "It's really you."

He said something she didn't quite hear and then he was kissing her. He kissed her for quite a long time, and when he finally raised his head, they were both shaking.

"It's really me," he said, his voice not quite under control.

She stared up into his face, drinking in the sight of him as a thirst-driven traveler might stare at an oasis. She touched his cheek and then his hair. It was damp with rain. "Did you get my letter?" she asked wonderingly.

His hands were still on her waist. "This morning. Ben flew me up."

"Ben! He doesn't have a license."

He removed one hand from her waist and slid it into her long black hair. "He just got it," he murmured.

"Oh, Leo," she said shakily. And he kissed her again.

It was ten minutes more before he finally took his trench coat off. Isabel went to hang it in the bathroom, and when she returned to the living room, he said, fiercely, "Do you know the hell you've put me through?"

"Yes, oh, yes." He was standing in front of the green velvet sofa. She stayed where she was in the doorway and gazed at him. She couldn't get enough of looking at him. "I've been through it myself," she said. "Bob says I've looked like grim death ever since I came home."

"Bob," said Leo. "Now there is a fellow whose hand I want to shake."

Isabel looked into the hall. "Where is he?" she asked, missing him for the first time.

"I reckon he's being tactful." Leo smiled and held out his hand. "Come and sit next to me," he said softly. "No sense in wastin' such thoughtfulness."

When Bob finally returned a half an hour later, he closed the front door with unnecessary force before he came into the living-room doorway. "Is it safe for me to return?" he asked the couple on the sofa.

Isabel laughed and got to her feet. "You poor thing. Come on in and be introduced."

"We met at the door, briefly," Bob said, and came

into the room. There was a guarded expression in his eyes as he looked at Leo, and Isabel suddenly realized that he was afraid of how Leo was going to react to him.

Leo grinned and held out his hand. "Very briefly. I had other things on my mind, I'm afraid. How do you do."

Bob shook hands composedly. "Do I offer you my congratulations, Senator?"

"You do. And call me Leo. After all, we're practically going to be brothers-in-law."

Bob's face relaxed slightly. "I'm so glad, Isabel," he said, and looked at her.

She was radiant. "So am I."

"I told her she owed it to you," Leo said amiably. "After all, you've housed her for years. We'll buy a nice big house and you can come for long visits."

Bob's face relaxed completely and he grinned. "*You* owe that to me," he said. "You're taking my cook."

"Yep. And I'm taking her right away, too." He looked at Isabel. "How would you like to come back to Charleston with me and be married?"

She sighed. "It sounds wonderful."

"Well," said Bob, "I have heard you're a man of action."

Leo chuckled.

"Where is Ben?" Isabel asked suddenly.

"We're staying at the Essex House. He can fly us home tomorrow."

"Great," said Isabel faintly. "Ben," she explained to Bob, "is Leo's brother. Leo's *young* brother. He just got his flying license."

"That's terrific."

"Yes, isn't it. Oh, well," Isabel said philosophically, "if we go down, at least we'll go down together."

"He's very good," Leo said firmly. "And now, since you have to pack, I'll be off. I'll pick you up tomorrow morning. At nine sharp."

"His ancestors were generals," Isabel said excusingly to Bob. "Both revolutionary and Confederate. He just can't help organizing."

Bob ignored her. "I'll make sure she's ready," he said to Leo. "And now, to add to my previously demonstrated tactfulness, I will retire and allow you to say good night alone."

"Bob," Isabel said, "you are a prince."

"I know," he returned modestly, and went off down the hall. Leo turned to Isabel.

"I'll see you tomorrow," he said softly.

"Yes." She looked up at him out of eyes that were wide and dark and unspeakably beautiful. "I love you so much," she said.

"I thought you meant it," he said. "That stuff about never marrying because of your art. I really thought you meant it."

"I thought I did, too," she replied softly.

He put his arms around her and held her close. "It made sense, you know." His cheek was against her hair. "It made such damn good sense."

"It might have made sense, but it wasn't true. You have to be open to life, Bob told me. And he was right. You have to live if you want to create. And without you, I don't seem to be any good at living."

"Well, I'm sure not any good at living without you." His voice sounded oddly husky.

Isabel closed her eyes. "I wish you didn't have to go."

"So do I, honey. So do I."

After a minute she pushed him away. "Well, you can tell you mother to book the church and hire the organist. All your old girlfriends can get out their handkerchiefs."

"Are you serious?" he asked. "Could you really stand a big wedding?"

"Leo, your mother's heart will be broken if we just stand up in front of the priest with a couple of witnesses."

A very slow smile started at the corners of his eyes. "True," he said.

"Would Paige like to be my maid of honor?"

The smile spread to his mouth. "She'd love it."

"Well, then . . ."

"One month," he said. "I'll give Mama one month. If she can't organize a wedding in that time, I'm going to drag you off by myself."

"She'll manage," said Isabel. "After all, she's a Sinclayeh."

"So she is," he murmured. "And so will you be too, honey." And he bent to kiss her again.

RAPTURE ROMANCE

**Provocative and sensual,
passionate and tender—
the magic and mystery of love
in all its many guises**

NEW TITLES AVAILABLE NOW

RAPTURE ROMANCE

*Provocative and sensual,
passionate and tender—
the magic and mystery of love
in all its many guises*

COMING NEXT MONTH

TOUCH THE SUN by JoAnn Robb. When aerial photographer Alinda Jamison agreed to work for Drew Fletcher, she knew the job came with risks even more dangerous than flying. One tender kiss from this patient, handsome man took her to heights of ecstasy she'd never dreamed possible. But love brought fear, too. . . . Could she survive a crash into heartbreak or was this love strong enough to soar forever. . . ?

A DREAM TO SHARE by Deborah Benét. Handsome Olympic champion Kell King wanted beautiful Orin O'Mally for his partner—to share his dream of becoming the world's best in professional pairs skating. Their fire on ice swept Orin into a dizzying spin of desire. But would falling in love be enough to melt a heart turned cold with a secret—and a fear—that could destroy her career. . . . and her chance with Kell?

HIDDEN FIRES by Diana Morgan. Gourmet food expert Allegra Russo was both enraged and enraptured by ruggedly handsome Mark Trackman, a confirmed male chauvinist. A business deal brought them into confrontation, and while his attitude toward working women infuriated her, his sweet kisses sparked a passion she couldn't deny. Allegra wanted Mark and his love, yet she was unsure if their professional differences would keep her from winning his heart. . . .

BROKEN PROMISES by Jillian Roth. Alison Mitchell was a genius with computers . . . but a failure with men. Badly scarred from a disastrous marriage, she buried herself in work, until Curt Ross swept into her life. The most sensuous man she'd ever met, his fiery kisses were irresistible. But even as the bond between them seemed to grow stronger, Ali wondered if she dare trust any man again—even Curt. . . .

RAPTURE ROMANCE

*Provocative and sensual,
passionate and tender—
the magic and mystery of love
in all its many guises*

Titles of Special Interest from RAPTURE ROMANCE

*Price is $2.25 in Canada
To order, please use coupon on last page.

RAPTURE ROMANCE

Provocative and sensual, passionate and tender— the magic and mystery of love in all its many guises

(0451)

RAPTURE ROMANCE

**Provocative and sensual,
passionate and tender—
the magic and mystery of love
in all its many guises**

**Buy them at your local
bookstore or use coupon
on next page for ordering.**

RAPTURE ROMANCE

Provocative and sensual, passionate and tender— the magic and mystery of love in all its many guises

RAPTURE ROMANCE

Provocative and sensual, passionate and tender— the magic and mystery of love in all its many guises

---

Buy them at your local bookstore or use coupon on next page for ordering.